SLEEPAWAY CAMP

a novel by
B R FLYNN

based on the original screenplay by
ROBERT HILTZIK

Encyclopocalypse Publications
www.encyclopocalypse.com

for all the Angelas

SLEEPAWAY CAMP

PROLOGUE

A MEMORY

The camp was empty. Deserted.

Once, some years ago now, Camp Arawak was teeming with kids—children as young as ten and as old as eighteen, all of them with their own idiosyncrasies, their own hang-ups, their own desires, their own triumphs and defeats. Now they were all gone, either grown or dead.

Their voices echoed like ghosts as the figure stepped carefully through the ruins of the camp, trespassing far past the signs posted out by the main road: KEEP OUT BY ORDER OF COUNTY SHERIFF. The figure gave these warnings no mind and explored the camp's lush grounds.

Places like this, off the beaten trail in upstate New York, die on the vine during the off-season. And now it was fall. The leaves had begun to turn. There was a chill in the air.

The figure longed for summer, longed for days past. They were searching for something that couldn't be recaptured. Something that was ephemeral. Something that had, at least in the figure's case, never really existed at all.

Sensing movement nearby, the figure turned and caught sight of a squirrel running off into the woods. The figure smiled and tried to keep up with the animal, but it was too fast.

Hanging back and watching the little creature pick out the right tree and run up it, the figure stood, hands on hips, and took in the sights and sounds of nature all around.

The air was pregnant with anticipation. It was as if Mother Nature herself was expecting something—trouble, perhaps, like the calm before a storm. The figure looked up at the sky. There were clouds up there, but they weren't gray. All of them were big, fluffy and white. They moved past the sun and bright rays illuminated the forest ground. In the undergrowth, something glinted in the sunlight, attracting the figure's attention.

Taking a few steps towards the glint of light, the figure frowned, squinted. When they were sure of what it was, they smiled and closed the distance, crouching down and picking up the object.

It was an old arrow. Obviously, it had been lost and left behind when the camp was operational. Though it was old and had spent some years out in the wild, its head was still sharp. Still brilliant in the sunlight.

The figure, smiling wide now, took the arrow by its shaft, pinching it between thumb and the first two fingers of their hand. Rolled it back and forth so that it twirled in the sunlight, kicking off brilliant beams.

"Are you ready to go?"

The voice came from behind, near the main road. The figure didn't need to turn to see who it was but did so anyway.

The man who had spoken stood sternly, hands crossed over his chest. He was big, beefy, and looked like he had been carved out of a particularly large side of pork. The figure smiled at him. Nodded. "Almost. Give me a few minutes."

They kept the arrow hidden from his sight. He was probably too far away to see it, but it was best not to take any chances. The big man would want the arrow for himself.

For the moment, he seemed satisfied. With a nod, he turned away and left the figure alone.

This was nothing new. They were always alone.

Even at camp.

The figure looked around once again. From this vantage point, they could see the cabins of the old camp. Beyond it, the lake. So much had happened there. Long ago.

In another life.

CHAPTER
ONE

DESTINY AT LAKE ALGONQUIN

1

July, 1975

Lake Algonquin was gorgeous in the summer. When the sun came up in the early morning and bathed the countryside with its brilliance, the water looked like undulating gold. By midday, with the sun high overhead, the lake was filled with tourists and locals alike, all of them spending their time and money basking in its glory.

With so much natural beauty, it was no wonder that so much industry had popped up around the lake in the last few decades. The east shore was near the interstate—it was all roads. But the south shore of the lake was lined with large cabins and houses, practically all of them available for rent during the summer months. To the west, a beautiful white beach dominated. Sunbathers dotted it like sea lions. And, finally, to the north was Camp Arawak, *the* destination for active boys and girls. The summer of '75 was shaping up to be one of the camp's best years.

John Baker wasn't thinking about Camp Arawak. At the

moment, he was simply enjoying spending time with his two children out on the water in their sailboat. The boat had been purchased when Judith, his wife, had still been alive. She had been gone some years now, and though he missed her, life was pretty good.

John looked at his children and smiled. Peter and Angela were twins, five years old—a playful pair. Both of them wore their life jackets. This was a hard rule of John's: if they wanted to be out on the water, they had to wear their life jackets, even if they were going to stay in the boat the whole time. It was simply common sense, in his opinion.

Casting an eye towards the south shore, John could see the house they had rented for the week. It was a big, white affair that looked out on the lake like an austere, rich uncle, though not unkind. He chuckled at the thought. Lenny was in the house at the moment. John's partner had drunk a little too much the night before and declined the offer to go out on the water for the morning.

No matter. They had lunch with Judith's sister coming up soon, and John would see Lenny then, which was enough.

"Cut it out!" Angela said.

John, who by now was just looking up at the sky at nothing in particular as he laid on the deck of the boat, looked at his children once again.

"Daddy," Angela pleaded, "tell him to leave me alone. Peter started it!"

"I did not, you liar!"

"Did not."

"Did too."

"Alright," John said, still not moving from his spot on the boat, "let's settle down and stop fighting."

"She started it," Peter said.

Somewhere not too far away from them, a motorboat whizzed by. A water skier trailed behind the boat on a tow rope.

John was a little annoyed by the noise. It broke the serene nature of the lake, but Peter seemed pretty interested.

"That looks neat," he said. "Can I try it, Daddy?"

John sat up now and gave the boy his best fake smile. He didn't like the idea of Peter getting anywhere near one of those boats, let alone being dragged by one and getting a faceful of exhaust. Still, he didn't want to upset the boy.

"Maybe in a couple of years," he said, "if we ever get a motorboat."

This was unlikely. John preferred the simple pleasures of a sailboat. There was something romantic about them. Lenny didn't quite share John's opinion on this, but he indulged him just the same, and he pretended to agree when John spoke about his fantasies to someday buy a *real* sailing boat, something that could take them all the way across the Atlantic.

Angela took a look over her shoulder at Camp Arawak before turning her earnest eyes on John. "Can we go to the camp? I bet they'd show us there."

Unbidden, John was flooded with memories of camp when he was a boy. How he had been relentlessly teased, taunted, beaten up. Somehow this seemed an even worse idea than being dragged behind a motorboat, and he couldn't keep a slight note of disapproval from his voice when he answered her. "Well, I don't know about that."

He stood up on the deck of the small sailboat and looked out towards camp, frowning. He hadn't gone to Camp Arawak, of course. The little slice of Hell he had frequented was called Camp Blackfoot, in New Jersey. But Camp Arawak seemed pretty similar. The docks looked the same and what he could make out of the cabins beyond the shore looked reasonably close enough.

He was imaging Peter at camp. What would the other boys make of him? Even at this age, the boy was already showing signs of how different he was compared to the other boys. John couldn't help but remember his own upbringing. He didn't want his children to grow up the way he had been raised—not allowing himself to be who he really was, something that had followed him into adulthood. However, had it been any different, he might never have had his two children.

In his musings, he was completely surprised when both of his children pushed him over the side of the sailboat. Balance completely thrown off now, the boat rocked, tipped and toppled over. It was a complete capsizing and both Peter and Angela were dunked into the water.

Taking a moment to make sure that they were okay—and seeing that they were—John laughed as he took hold of the underside of the boat, which was now the topside.

"Oh," he said, "you think that's funny, huh? You little schemers!"

Both of his children were laughing along with him. They splashed in the water, play fighting, and John couldn't remember the last time he had enjoyed himself this much— certainly never with his children.

The motorboat whizzed by them again, but this time John barely noticed it. He was having too good of a time at the moment. They weren't in any real danger, anyway. The sailboat was—or *had been*, as the case may be—close to shore. Surely a motorboat wouldn't get as close to shore as they were.

"Hey John, we gotta go meet the Doc!"

It was Lenny. John looked towards shore and saw his partner smiling back at him. Lenny tapped his watch and spoke up again. "It's almost One. Doc's gonna be here soon!"

The man was right. They had to get out of the water soon or they would be late meeting Dr Martha Thomas, his late wife's sister. He waved to Lenny to show the man that he understood, then turned to Peter and Angela. "Come on, fellas. Dr Thomas is on her way up."

"Aunt Martha's coming?" Angela said.

"Is Ricky coming, too?" Peter asked.

Ricky was Martha's son. "No, I'm afraid he's spending the

weekend with his father." John liked Martha, but he wasn't surprised that her marriage hadn't lasted all that long. She was an odd duck.

2

It was pretty clear to Craig that Delores wasn't having a good time. She was a nice enough girl, he supposed, but she was a bit of a stick in the mud. Mary Ann, on the other hand, was more of Craig's type. Bubbly, blonde, and fun. Just the way he liked them.

The three of them were in one of the camp's motorboats. More accurately, Craig and Mary Ann were in the motorboat. Delores was being dragged behind it on a pair of rickety skies. Craig couldn't quite see her face, but he knew that she was not enjoying herself at all.

Craig was a counselor at Camp Arawak for the summer. This was his second year there and it had been a busy one. He was on lifeguard duty and had used his position—and considerable charm—to coax Mary Ann out on the boat with him. She had insisted that Delores come along, which was fine by him... he supposed.

How Mary Ann had persuaded Delores onto the waterboard, Craig had no idea. But she had and now they were out on the water enjoying the midday sun. Well, Mary Ann was enjoying herself. Delores wasn't, and neither was Craig. He was worried that he was going to get in trouble. He wasn't supposed to be out this long with the campers. But really, he shouldn't be worrying. No one would miss them.

"Hang in there, Delore!" Mary Ann called out to her friend trailing behind them at the end of the rope. "You're doing great!"

Delores called back, but Craig couldn't quite hear her over the roar of the engine. It wasn't hard to see that she didn't want to be out on the water anymore, though. She was a funny one.

Always worried about something, always with a sour look on her face.

"Hey," Mary Ann said. "How about letting me take the wheel, huh?"

He scoffed, shook his head. "Come on. You know I can't do that."

"Don't be such a stiff. I know how to drive these things. My old man's got one twice as big."

He believed it. Mary Ann came from money. Most of the campers did. Camp Arawak was a getaway for rich kids for the summer. It wasn't exactly upscale, but it was expensive for a summer camp. And, based on what he'd heard, Mary Ann's father was one of the richest men in the state. Still, he couldn't let her drive the boat. He turned to look her in the eye. "Yeah, and is your old man gonna give me a job when I get fired?"

"Oh, come on, lighten up. No one's gonna see us way out here." Pleading with him now. She put a hand on his leg. Smiled. She sure was cute. No, more than cute. Dynamite. "Come on. Please." Those pouty lips.

Craig melted. "Alright."

"Super."

As they switched places, Craig couldn't help but savor the feel of Mary Ann's skin. Her legs brushed past his own as she got into the driver's seat. His attention wavered as he fantasized about that skin. It took him a moment to regain some semblance of control. "Just for a minute, okay?"

She nodded as she took the wheel and settled into place. Immediately, she revved the engine. The motorboat lurched forward, breaking over a wake.

"Not too fast!" Craig said, but she wasn't listening.

He looked out behind the boat to make sure that they hadn't lost Delores, but no such luck. She was still out there, looking like a drowned cat.

Apparently, Mary Ann saw her differently. She, too, was looking behind the boat at her friend, and she called out to her, "You look like a skiing hunchback! Straighten up, will ya?!"

Craig chuckled at that. He calmed down a little. They really were far out from the camp. No one would see them out here. They could have a little fun. Where was the harm in that?

Delores was yelling now, but Craig couldn't hear her at all. She looked frantic, almost crazed. What was wrong with her?

"What'd she say?" Mary Ann asked.

"I don't know."

Neither of them were looking ahead. Mary Ann was looking at her friend and Craig was looking at Mary Ann. He was imagining what it would be like to kiss her. Wondering what she tasted like.

Idly, still inside his head, Craig turned to look ahead, to the bow of the ship. He was alarmed at how close they were to the south shore of the lake. And there was something else. He could see a white shape ahead of them. Something in the water. It took him a moment to realize that it was a sailboat. A small, capsized sailboat. There were people in the water near it. Three people. Two of them were children.

Now he understood that Delores was trying to warn them.

"There's a boat!" she screamed. "We're going to hit them!"

"Holy shit!" Craig said. "Turn off the motor! Turn the wheel! Turn it!"

He wanted to push Mary Ann aside, wanted to take control of the boat, but he was worried that she would be hurt if she was suddenly knocked out of the boat at this speed. He had to rely on her in this crucial moment.

3

Standing on shore, Lenny had ringside seats to an event in Hell. Prime location to witness his life suddenly change forever.

The motorboat charged towards the capsized sailboat and the forms of John, Peter and Angela. The pilot of the motorboat had tried to turn at the last moment, but it was too late. The motorboat was going to hit the figures in the water.

He saw John scrambling, saw him try to push his children out of the way. His desperate act of self-sacrifice was only partially successful.

The motorboat surged towards them like some leviathan from the depths. It seemed to pounce on them. It hit Angela first, the bow of the motorboat slamming into her skull. Lenny was too far away to hear it, but he could easily imagine the horrid crack as her head was smashed open. The girl was gone and out of sight now, under the waves as the motorboat kept moving. It was upon John next, the bulk of the ship hitting him in the side as he frantically struggled to get away.

Lenny saw his partner's left arm torn asunder. John was trapped between the underside of the capsized sailboat and the roaring motorboat.

As the motorboat vaulted over the capsized sailboat, it spun John around like a top, whirling and twirling until his face came into contact with the spinning blades of the outboard motor. His head turned to mulch—a sickening squelch of hair and thick red sprayed across the pure white of the sailboat.

Peter had been tossed clear of the passing motorboat. But as the boat mounted the capsized vessel and hit the water on the other side, the girl who had been water skiing behind it fanned out wide as the motorboat turned. Her left ski slammed into Peter's head and threw the boy towards shore.

Lenny stood frozen in place. The horror was too much for him. He was only able to utter one word. It was barely audible over the roar of the motorboat engine. "John."

Finally, the fatal boat came to rest, floating in the water near the capsized sailboat. The water skier was screaming as she bobbed up and down in the waves close to the carnage.

"Oh my God!" she said. "Somebody help them quick! Please help them! We hit them all! We killed them! Please, somebody help them!"

But there was no help to be had. Lenny's muscles seemed locked in place. He couldn't believe what he had just seen. Never before had he seen so much blood. So much death.

Peter was still alive, treading water with the help of his life jacket. It was a miracle that he hadn't been knocked unconscious. After another moment, the screaming girl swam to the boy's side, her face full of tears that mixed with the water of the gorgeous, serene lake.

4

"Now, how is my little angel feeling?" Dr. Martha Thomas said.

Peter Baker couldn't seem to lift his head high enough to look at his aunt. The bandages that were wrapped around his skull seemed to weigh a ton, and he hung his head, seemingly interested more in his shoes than his aunt.

It had been two weeks since the accident at the lake. Peter had spent that entire time in the hospital and a recovery center. Though he was young, and he didn't understand all the details, he knew that adults had spoken seriously about him and his situation, paperwork had been signed, and now he would be living with his aunt and his cousin, Ricky. He had no idea why he couldn't stay with Lenny, which is what he really wanted.

"There's no need to worry," Aunt Martha said, sensing his discomfort and melancholy. "I will take great care of you. Yes, I'm quite certain that I will."

They stood in the front room of Aunt Martha's house in Hudson Falls. While it wasn't a mansion by any stretch of the imagination, it was a large house and was no doubt expensive. Even Peter knew this. Aunt Martha herself was bright and larger-than-life. Peter had never seen such bold colors on an adult before. Whenever they had visited, he joked to his cousin that he had to shield his eyes from his aunt's outfit.

On this day, her choice of green was like an exclamation

point, an announcement to the world that she was here and would be dealt with. Circling Peter like a shark sensing prey, her smile was plastered on her face. Peter concentrated on his shoes. He was listening to her—he supposed that he would *have* to listen to her from now on—but he didn't want to look at her. Her crazy colors and the unimaginable loss he had suffered made him want to curl up in bed and sleep for the rest of his life.

"Now," she continued, "as a doctor, I know that living here will be an adjustment for you. There will be changes. Changes by the yard!"

From Peter's shoe-gazing vantage point, he could see that Aunt Martha had a number of large bags by her side. They looked to be from an expensive store. The bags were bright pink. *Are those for me?* Peter thought with a frown. He couldn't help but be intrigued, though. Following quickly on from this thought was another: *Changes? What changes?*

"But isn't life all about change?" Aunt Martha said. "Why I'm told that there are frogs that change their sex when the need arises. *Frogs and fish!* Isn't that interesting?" She paused, looked away into the middle distance and raised one hand to her face, her index finger resting on her chin. She seemed to be considering some strange equation in her head. When she spoke, it was seemingly to herself. "We live in a strange world." Then the plastered-on, mannequin smile returned and she looked at Peter. "But life persists, as I always say! Oh, you're going to enjoy living with us so much! Yes, I know you are."

She reached into one of the bags at her feet. Since this was where Peter was looking, he observed her hands. It was as if her actions were rehearsed. There was a strange mannerism to her movements, to the way she spoke. This wasn't exactly news to Peter—this was how she had always been—but this little moment, this small observation of her hands reaching into that pink bag, seemed to bring it into focus for him.

Aunt Martha pulled a girl's dress out of the bag. To Peter, it looked like a dress that one would put on a doll. She held it out in front of her so he could get a better look at it. Peter continued to observe the floor.

"As a welcome-home present I bought you such wonderful new clothes," Aunt Martha said.

These clothes were for him? It didn't compute in Peter's head. Did she expect him to wear this dress? To wear all the clothes in the big pink bag? Why? What was going on here? He was a boy—he wasn't supposed to wear clothes like this.

And yet...

He remembered looking through his sister's clothes. Remembered running his hand along them. They were so soft. Gentle. Wasn't it true that he wished that he could wear them?

"I just hope that Richard doesn't get jealous that I didn't get him anything. Oh, but then he is such a dear. I'm sure that he won't mind." She had another one of her "moments"—as Peter was beginning to think of them—and raised that index finger to her chin once again. Looked off into the middle distance. "No, I'm sure he won't."

This "moment" lasted longer this time, her stare seeming to pierce the wall and the yard past it until it penetrated the very fabric of the universe itself. Peter was about to nudge her, try to get her restarted, when she snapped out of it. Smiled again.

"You see," she explained, "I've always wanted a little girl."

So there it was. Peter was beginning to understand. She wanted him to be a girl. Part of him was afraid—was, in fact screaming inside—but another part of him was calm and collected. Accepting, even. In a perverse way, it seemed natural. He had always admired his sister, had looked up to her, and hadn't part of him—a big but secret part—wanted to be like her? Hadn't he wanted to be a girl like her?

"But of course, when my husband left..." she continued before trailing off, no doubt staring off into space once again before resetting. "Oh, well! That's all water under the bridge, as

I always say. Water under the bridge." Enunciating each word like she was teaching a class.

Tuning her out ever so slightly, Peter started thinking of a new name for himself. Peter wouldn't do if he was going to be a girl now, so what would be a good name? What would fit? Penelope? That didn't exactly roll off the tongue, did it?

"But it certainly will be a nice little surprise when Richard comes home to find a little girl in the house," his aunt rattled on. "Yes, I've always dreamed of a little girl just like you. I mean, we already have a boy, so another one simply would not do. Oh, no, absolutely not."

Her excitement grew. Peter could see her shifting her weight from one foot to the next, as if she couldn't stand still. "A little girl would be so much nicer. Don't you think so, Angela?"

At that, Peter finally looked up at her, perplexed. For a moment, he had lost her. He resisted the urge to look behind him—he had a childish notion that his aunt was speaking to the ghost of his dead sister. Finally it dawned on him that she was still speaking to him. But why had she called him Angela?

Aunt Martha went into another one of her moments, looking off into nothingness, speaking to the air as much as to Peter. "Angela... Such a lovely name." She looked at him again with a terrible smile. "Why, I believe it means 'angel.' Why, yes, I'm sure it does. I know you're going to like that name. Won't you, Peter? Oh, I do apologize, *Angela*."

The revelation came upon him: not only did his aunt expect him to live as a girl now, she expected him to literally *be* Angela. To take over for his dead sister, to step into her shoes and prance around pretending to be her. Peter suddenly had an image of himself puppeting the water-logged corpse of his sister on a stage, the audience full of laughing, clapping dead men. The whole situation struck him as almost impossibly ghoulish.

He looked up into the face of his aunt and saw madness. Pure, unfiltered insanity. He supposed that he always knew this about her on some level, but he had never truly confronted it before now. His aunt was not only eccentric but completely mad. And now he would have to live with her for the rest of his childhood.

And she wanted him to be Angela.

But what could he do? He had to listen to her, didn't he? Had to obey her? She was an adult and he was only a child. Surely he had to do what she told him to do, didn't he? Slowly, he nodded, sealing his fate.

From that moment on, Peter was no longer a he, was no longer even Peter. She was Angela.

Angela Baker resurrected.

5

"Mommy, look at that weird girl!"

Angela—the *new* Angela—looked up from the lemonade stand she and Ricky had erected in front of Aunt Martha's house. In fact, it had been five years since the accident that had taken away her sister and father and turned her into the girl she was today, ten years-old and pretty in an odd sort of way. It was a warm summer day—the perfect day to sell some lemonade to the fine people of Hudson Falls.

It was a boy who had spoken. He stood across the street from Aunt Martha's house, one hand holding onto an adult woman the other pointing accusingly at Angela. His small, bright eyes seemed to bore into her, and Angela felt herself grow small, withdrawn. Suddenly the lemonade stand seemed like a horrible idea. Horrible, because it meant that people were going to be looking at her, judging her.

"Stop that," the mother chided her child. "It's rude to point."

She hurried him along, giving Angela a small, forced, apologetic smile. Ricky came out of the house cradling an armful of dixie cups. Ricky Thomas was older than Angela by more than two years. He had dark hair like his cousin, but it tended more towards the brown end of the spectrum in contrast to Angela's black. He was nicely tanned, having just come back from Camp Arawak the day before. It had been a hard year for Ricky. His father died earlier in the year in a freak accident, and he had been spending a lot of time with his cousin since then.

Ricky caught sight of the troubled condition of his cousin, looked across the street and immediately figured out the situation. Dropping the dixie cups onto the table of the lemonade stand, he stormed out onto the sidewalk, called after the mother and son. "Hey, leave my cousin alone! Get out of here, why don't you?!"

The mother looked back in shock, but the boy didn't even turn his head. Ricky planted both hands on his hips and put a serious look on his face. The mother shook her head.

"Mind your manners, young man!" she called back to him. Before Ricky could answer, she shuffled her son down a connecting street, out of view.

Ricky turned back to his cousin and sighed. Angela's head was bowed. She was looking at her feet once again. When Ricky had reached her, he put a hand on her shoulder. That got her to look up.

He smiled down at her. His smile was as warm as his touch and Angela found herself smiling back in spite of herself. Peter had agreed to do this with her, which was nice. He could be out playing with his friends on such a nice, warm, summer day, but he had chosen to spend it with her, his weird little cousin.

A small moment of silence passed. Finally, Ricky looked at her again. "I'm sure mom will let you come next year."

Before he had left for the summer camp, he had tried to convince Aunt Martha to let Angela go, too. She had insisted that Angela was too young for Camp Arawak. Three weeks without any parents around? No, it wouldn't do, not with such a young, vulnerable girl.

Angela, for her part, didn't really want to go to camp. She

didn't like the idea of being around all those other kids. They would look at her.

Judge her.

But Ricky was still on about it. He always wanted to spend time with her. It was nice of him. Since Angela was home-schooled, she didn't interact with any other kids besides Ricky. They didn't go out much, either. Only to the movies from time to time and out to eat when the mood struck Aunt Martha.

"The other kids will like you," Ricky said, as if reading her mind. "I mean, you're a little different, but you're not weird. You're just quiet."

She looked at him, eyebrows raised. They rarely spoke about what exactly made Angela different from the other girls. Though Ricky knew about Angela's secret, he almost never brought it up. He certainly never called her by any name other than Angela.

Ricky looked away and kept his mouth shut. The sun was in his eyes, but he pretended like it didn't bother him. Angela reached out and put a hand on his shoulder. Ricky smiled and took hold of her hand and held it tight. He nodded emphatically.

"Yeah," he said, "next year for sure. She'll let you go next year."

But he was wrong. It was another three years before Aunt Martha let Angela go to sleepaway camp.

6

July, 1983

On the morning that Angela finally went to Camp Arawak, she found a snake in the backyard of the house. It was one of those summer mornings where it wasn't too hot but the sun was blinding. Angela had been dreading this day and she got up earlier than anyone else in the household, made herself a bowl of cereal, ate it, and went out back to just sit and try not to think about anything.

Aunt Martha had a little garden against one wall of the house. It sat in the shadow of a large tree. The garden wasn't much, but it was nice and Angela liked to sit next to it some mornings. She liked to listen to the birds and the bugs that came out during the summer months. Liked the idea of life all about her, creatures that she could hardly ever see but knew were there.

Despite not wanting to, she was thinking about camp. Thinking about all those other kids. All those strangers. How would they treat her?

Her gaze fixed on some point on the fence that set out Aunt Martha's property. It was a full acre of land so the fence was quite some distance away from the garden, but Angela could see every detail of it with clarity. A beetle was currently struggling its way up the wooden slats. A bird sat on the top of the fence. To Angela, it looked like the bird was eying the bug, waiting for the right moment to strike.

She was so distracted, her mind elsewhere, that she didn't notice the snake when it slithered out of the little garden and approached her. It got within an inch of her hand before she saw it.

With a little yelp, she scuttled away from the creature. The snake was a dull green. It was small, thin, almost certainly harmless, but it scared her just the same.

And yet she was also fascinated by it.

Where had it come from? She couldn't remember seeing one like it before. Was it some neighborhood pet that had escaped its enclosure?

Angela cautiously approached the snake and got down on her hands and knees to get a better look at it. The creature's tongue flicked in and out of its mouth, tasting the air. The girl's mind conjured up giant snakes of the imagination. Killer snakes from some kind of pulp story. A cobra, maybe, like the one in

Raiders of the Lost Ark. That movie had scared her, but she had also loved it. There had been *tons* of snakes in that one.

Yes, it was fascinating. But it had also scared her and she was angry at it for that. She narrowed her eyes and watched the snake as it made its way into the yard.

Angela wanted nothing more than to stay here and study the snake, but she didn't have the time. She had to get upstairs and dress for camp. Aunt Martha had made it clear that she wanted both of them to wear their Camp Arawak t-shirts. Ricky said that this was a stupid idea, but both he and Angela knew that he would do what he was told. So she had to change.

7

"Hurry, sweeties," Martha called from the bottom of the stairs. "We don't want to miss the bus!"

Even from the top of the stairs, as he rounded the newel post and started down the steps, Ricky could see that his mother was in one of her loopy, not-all-there moods this morning. Enthusiastic as she was, she still had that strange distracted air about her, as if she were living in two worlds at the same time. She didn't even appear to realize that he and Angela were already on their way down. She paused, one finger to her chin and looking off into the middle distance somewhere. "Goodness, no. That wouldn't do at all."

Once she had snapped out of it, she called out again, not even bothering to look up. "Richard. Angela." Finally, it seemed to dawn on her that they were already practically on top of her as they reached the bottom of the stairs. "Oh, here you are."

Ricky gave her the best smile that he was capable of on a summer morning when, by all rights, he should be sleeping in. Angela was reserved and quiet, so no different than usual. Martha put a quick, soft hand on Ricky's shoulder, gave him a plastic smile of her own before reaching down to grab a paper bag from the floor. She handed it to him.

"Look what I did," she said. "I packed you and your cousin some goodies for the ride up to camp. Wasn't that nice of me, hmm?"

Ricky had trouble even looking at the contents of the bag, it was so overstuffed with food. A few apples sat on top. Under that, Ricky could see carrots and celery wrapped in plastic like fresh corpses in body bags. He sighed. "Any chips?"

"Why, of course. I believe that there's a whole bag." Then she was gone again, off looking away from them, hand to her chin. Ricky saw that she had tied a red string around her index finger. This was her little way of reminding herself not to forget some task. Ricky had no intention of asking her about it.

"Why I'm almost certain of it," she said to herself.

Ricky pushed gently past her, heading to the front door. When Angela stepped off the stairs, Martha was on her like a hawk, hands reaching out to take hold of the girl. She tugged at Angela's shoulder-length hair, smiled. This smile was more genuine than the one she had given Ricky. Though he wouldn't admit it to anyone else, Ricky was a little jealous of his mother's affection for, and attention given to, Angela.

"Angela," she said, "isn't there anything special my little girl would care for, hmm?"

Ricky rolled his eyes and sighed once again. "We gotta go, mom. It's getting late."

Though he couldn't actually hear the bus pulling up outside the house, he could imagine it in his mind. It was true that he didn't like getting up so early on a summer morning, but he was eager to get to camp all the same. It was just about his favorite place in the world. Admittedly, it would be different this year with Angela coming for the first time, but he was posi- tive to make it a good experience for his cousin. He would protect her no matter what happened.

Martha and Angela joined him by the front door. She reached out in an extravagant gesture and put a hand on each of their shoulders. "Well of course you do, dear. We wouldn't want them to leave without you, now would we?" Another tiny moment of disconnectedness. "No, I'm afraid that wouldn't do at all." All at once, she was back, smiling once again. "Come, children. Let's be on our way."

She started with them towards the door but stopped, looking at the two of them with some concern. Ricky's temper was beginning to rise. Why wouldn't she just let them go?!

"Now what?" he said.

"I believe that I've forgotten something," she said. "Now what could it be?" The look of concern cleared from her face, and she came alive, like a puppet finally given life by a ventriloquist. "Oh, I remember what it is! I knew I would forget. I just kept reminding myself. In fact, I tied a string around..." She raised her hand and beamed at the red string around her index finger. "Around my finger, so I wouldn't forget!" She displayed it for both of them. "See? And I didn't." Distracted again—elsewhere. "You never can be too careful." She paused, a robot rebooting, mouthed, "Oh," to herself.

"Well, what is it?" Ricky said, unable to hide the frustration in his voice.

His mother didn't seem to notice at all. "Just a moment! I'll be right back!"

When she ran off into the house, Ricky shared a look with his cousin. He didn't have to say anything to her, his look said it all, *Mom's in one of her moods again.* Angela didn't say anything back, but she didn't have to, either.

Martha returned with a small packet of papers. She handed them to Ricky. "Here they are, all filled out and signed by yours truly. Wasn't that nice of me, hmm?"

Ricky flicked through the papers. He recognized his name, as well as Angela's, but the rest of it might as well have been written in Greek for all he could determine. "What are they?"

"Why, they're your physicals, of course," she explained. "We can't go to camp without our physicals, now can we?"

We. Our. It was as if she were coming to camp with them.

For a moment, Ricky imagined it, conjuring up the image of his mother at Camp Arawak. It was a comical and absurdly terrifying thought and he banished it from his mind as quickly as it came to him.

It was a good thing she had remembered the physicals, he admitted to himself. Since he wasn't going to point out the red string, they might have gotten all the way to camp before realizing that they didn't have them. That would have meant returning home.

"Just be sure not to tell anyone how you got them," she continued. "Oh, no, I'm afraid that they wouldn't approve of that at all. Even though they know that I am a doctor!"

She seemed proud of this to an absurd degree, beaming big and bright at the both of them. Ricky nodded with complete understanding. He had to make sure that he did his part to conceal Angela's secret. Angela would have the harder job, of course, showering away from the other girls, doing her best to keep her secret, but he was determined to make it as easy as possible for her.

But still…

Wasn't going to camp just about having fun? Why did he have the responsibility of taking care of his cousin? Of keeping her secret? Couldn't he just have fun? He looked at Angela. She was looking back at him, quiet as always, but with love in her eyes. He sighed for a third time that morning and put a hand on her shoulder. She managed a small smile in return.

"No matter what they do," he said to her, "I'll never tell."

"Oh, you're such a dear," Martha said. "Well, run along now."

"So long, Mom."

He grabbed both of their bags which had been set down beside the door. They left the house just in time. The bus was pulling up at the curb. He and Angela hurried along.

"I hope you have a good time," Martha called after them.

"But of course you will. Take good care of my little girl, Richard!"

They both waved goodbye to her as they ran to catch the bus. Ricky could hardly contain his excitement. Pretty soon he would be at camp! And he was going to make it the best summer ever for Angela.

Even if it killed him.

8

When the children had gone, Aunt Martha shut the door behind them and wandered aimlessly through the house. Eventually, she headed out back and stared at the sky for a moment. It was a bright, almost blinding morning. She had to shield her eyes from the sun.

When she turned to regard her little garden, she frowned. Something had disturbed her tranquil repose. Something small and slithery.

It was a snake.

For a moment, she was frightened. A snake, here in her garden! After this came the realization that the creature was dead.

With some caution, she approached it. Bent over to examine it closely. Yes, the small snake was dead alright.

Someone had stepped on it, crushing its skull to a bloody pulp.

CHAPTER
TWO

CAMP ARAWAK

1

Summer. It was the most magic word in a child's vocabulary.

For children, summers in this part of New York state were dominated by sleepaway camps just like Camp Arawak. Idyllic, green, preferably with a light, cool breeze wafting off a lake or river. Camp Arawak sat in gorgeous country some miles from Hudson Falls. On the first morning of the summer that would change everything, several busloads of kids pulled up to the camp and let loose their cargo of screaming, running, jumping, and cavorting live flesh.

Spilling from the buses, the kids looked like spawning salmon. They flooded the camp with their presence. This would be their home for the next three weeks, and they treated it as such.

Mel Kostic watched the kids as they ran into the camp—his camp—from the window of his office. He shook his head. He was pushing sixty and was already starting to waste away. His hair was turning white and his skin was getting that stretched-out, worn look that almost everyone who reaches their final days gets. He had the look of a shady character, someone you would expect to be running a carpet business that was actually a mob front instead of a summer camp upstate.

Taking a long drag on his cigar, he watched the kids as they hit Camp Arawak like a wave. *Why am I still doing this?*

There was a knock on his office door. He told the interloper to come, but didn't turn to regard him: he knew who it was.

"Ready to say hello to the kids?" Ronnie asked.

"Ready to survive another damn summer," Mel said. "Maybe."

Finally, he turned to Ronnie and gave the younger man a smile. Ronnie returned it. As head counselor and, in essence, Mel's right hand man, Ronnie had to keep in shape. The twenty-something young man was practically a bodybuilder. His dark hair was a little long for Mel's taste, but a lot of the young guys had long hair these days. Holdover from the sixties, Mel supposed.

Ronnie held a clipboard in his hands and he gave it a quick flick before turning to leave the office. Mel stopped him before he could make his exit. "Ask you a question?"

"Of course."

Mel took another drag of his cigar, gestured with his free hand. "Why am I still here?"

Ronnie looked concerned. He took a seat near the desk opposite Mel. "This is your place. Your passion."

"Passion?" Mel looked out the window at the kids streaming in. "Never really thought about it that way. It's okay money."

"But not *great* money," Ronnie said.

"No, not great."

"So it must be a passion of some kind, right?"

"I suppose so." Mel seemed frozen in place for a moment. He fell silent, and Ronnie didn't interrupt him for a second.

"Something wrong?"

"Doc says my liver ain't so good," Mel sighed. "Says I should take it easy. Too much stress."

"Your liver? That sounds more like the drink than the stress."

Mel shrugged. "One thing leads to the other."

"Aren't I always telling you to lay off that stuff?" Ronnie asked.

Mel gave him a dismissive wave of his free hand. Sighed again. Ronnie stood up from the chair and approached his boss. Put a hand on his shoulder. Looked him dead in the eye.

"You live for this," he said. "Every summer's when you come alive. Believe me, I can tell."

"Don't give me that greeting card crap," Mel said, but he was smiling now.

"Now you ready to go meet those kids?"

Mel nodded. "Ready as I'll ever be. Let's go."

"That's what I like to hear."

They left the office and headed out into the blinding sunlight to meet the kids. There was much shouting, waving, directing frantic children to the right cabins, but they would get it done. It was simply what they did.

2

As assistant cook at Camp Arawak for more summers than he could imagine, Ben had learned one lesson the hard way. When your superior acted in a way that was, perhaps, inappropriate at best, it was better to just laugh it off. To move on. To forget about it.

But, Lord, was it hard when your superior was someone like Artie.

On the day that the kids arrived at the camp, Ben was standing outside the rec hall—off the side kitchen door—among his colleagues. They had three helpers this year, a step up from last year when they got by with only one for most of the summer. College kids just looking for a little extra cash to put in their pockets. Artie was large, both wide and tall, forty years old, with the kind of haircut and that particular brand of facial hair that screamed Suspicious. Loud enough to hear the capital S.

At the moment, Artie watched the kids with a kind of glee that Ben always dreaded at the beginning of each summer. One summer, six years ago now, there had been some unpleasant business that had been hushed up. Ben didn't know the details, but he knew that it wasn't good.

But Artie was still here. Artie was still in charge. He had fried up some bacon just before the kids had arrived and ate it, piece by piece, with his hands as if filling up for some unimaginable task. The man's hands were greasy and he rubbed them together as he watched the children.

Ben could only shake his head and smile as wide as he could. There was nothing else to be done. Even though he was older than Artie by more than three decades, Artie was the one in charge. Had always been. What could you do? You smiled and laughed it off. Like always.

A group of kids went running by them, heading to the front entrance of the rec hall and Ben saw Artie visibly twitch, as if having a small orgasm triggered by their mere presence alone. The big man sighed, reached down and plucked a long strand of grass from the ground. It was between his teeth when he stood back up. He chewed on it like a cow.

"Look at all that young, fresh chicken," he said with clear admiration. He glanced at Ben, taking him in like a confidante. "Where I come from we call them 'baldies'."

Where do you come from? Ben thought. *Just where the Hell are you from, Artie? And who's this "we"?*

"Makes your mouth water, don't it?" Artie continued.

What Ben wanted to do was punch the motherfucker in the nose, drop him like a sack of potatoes. What he did was smile, shake his head, said, "Artie. They're too young to even understand what's on your mind."

Artie scoffed. "Too young? Ain't no such thing, old pal. You're just too old."

And that was Ben's cue to laugh it off. He laughed. It was his cue to forget about it. He waved a dismissive hand in Artie's direction. It was his cue to leave. He walked away from his fellow kitchen staff, heading inside. Here, in the kitchen, things made more sense. He understood things here. Had, in fact, been cooking his whole life. He knew every utensil here, every pot and every ingredient. More than Artie, certainly.

He breathed deep, the aroma of the kitchen filling his nostrils, and felt every day of his seventy-one years. He felt old, stretched out, used up. When he was a boy, in the early decades of the century, he did anything to survive—did what all children of color who lack the privilege of a comfortable upbringing. He scrapped. He entertained. He said, "Yes, sir, how high, sir?"

He laughed and forgot about it.

Camp Arawak might have looked like it was out of the world, might have looked like it was a retreat from the hustle and bustle, but it was like any other place. It had its hierarchies, it had its prejudices, it had its bullies.

And it had its predators.

Men like Artie.

But what could he do about it? Artie was the boss in this kitchen. His word was law. It was better to laugh it off. To move on.

And if it hurt sometimes—hurt in a real, tangible way—well then, that was the way of the world. He wasn't strong enough to change it.

Ben could hear laughter outside. It was the college kids, laughing at some off-color joke that Artie had made, no doubt. Ben worked up a smile and got to work. Work was all that mattered.

That, at least, was what he told himself.

3

Already, there were too many people.

Angela tried not to look any of them in the eye as they rushed past her and Ricky, all of them seemingly in a great hurry to get to their cabins, or to the rec hall, or to anywhere. She concentrated on the ground, on the trees and brush all around. It looked beautiful here, but there could be bugs, or snakes, hiding in the underbrush.

She cast a wary eye at Ricky, by her side as always. Despite her trepidation, his presence comforted her, which was good. She supposed that he would always be by her side.

And yet...

He already seemed distracted, anxious to leave her and rush off with the rest of the kids. Ricky kept casting longing glances at the others, at the lake, at the archery range. Angela worried that he would flee, just run off and disappear with the rest of the kids, leaving her alone. What would she do then?

Angela looked up at the sky and had to shade her eyes. The sun was blinding. When she looked back down, she jumped as a boy violated her personal space, sneaking up on them from behind and grabbing Ricky by the shoulders.

He was an attractive boy with blond hair and a pleasant face. At the moment a big smile was planted on it. He was obviously very pleased with himself for scaring the two of them.

"Hey Paul!" Ricky said, his momentary anger won over by recognition.

"Ricky!" Paul said. "They let you back again this year, huh?"

"Yeah," Ricky nodded.

"What's been going on? You winning?"

"Ah, you know. Same old shit." He looked past Paul at Angela, seeming to remember that she was there, too. Gesturing towards her, he introduced them. "Paul, this is my cousin, Angela. Angela, this my friend Paul."

She remembered hearing Ricky talk about Paul. It was clear

that Ricky thought highly of his friend and Angela could see why. Paul was cute and, though he was the same age as Ricky, he was already taller than his friend. Angela tried to meet his gaze but couldn't do it. She raised her head to look up at him briefly before looking down and away from him, saying nothing.

There was an awkward pause as Paul didn't understand what was happening. He looked at Ricky for answers, frowning.

"She's shy," Ricky explained. "First time away from home." Sighed. "I gotta show her where her bunk is. I'll catch you down the hill later."

"Great," Paul said. He made to leave, heading down the hill towards a cluster of cabins that were clearly the boys' bunks. After a moment, he stopped and looked back, seeming to remember something important. "Wait till you see Judy," he called out to Ricky, cupping his hands towards his chest as if he had large, squeezable breasts. "Man, oh man!"

"Oh yeah?" Ricky said, a wicked smile on his face.

"You'll see," Paul said and went about his business.

Ricky and Angela broke off from the wave of boys that were heading in the same direction as Paul towards a group of cabins higher up on the hill. This was where the reality of it all began to set in for Angela. Ricky was going to leave her. He was going to drop her off at one of the girls' cabins and head to his own bunk further down the hill. Real fear began to creep up on her as she imagined being alone among a cabin full of girls—strangers. It was almost too much to bear. *What am I going to do?!*

"Me and Judy were going steady here last year," Ricky said, as if Angela cared at all about the subject. She barely heard him, all of her attention fixed on the imminent terror of her situation.

"You'll probably be in the same cabin as her," Ricky continued. He gave her the layout of the camp. They were near the rec hall. Beside them was a shack for head councilor Ronnie and a slightly larger cabin for the camp's owner, Mel. The girls' bunks were a little further down the hill from there. Beyond that was the archery range and thick forest. Further down the hill were the boys' bunks and the lake.

Angela had a hard time taking it all in. Even though the camp wasn't all that large, she was already confused. She still couldn't get her current predicament out of her head. She was going to be abandoned soon, left to defend herself. But when Ricky said, "There she is," Angela snapped out of it long enough to look where he was pointing.

"Hey, Judy!" Ricky called out.

Standing near one of the cabins among a group of older boys—some of them might have even been counselors instead of campers—was an almost impossibly beautiful young woman. She looked towards them when Ricky called out. Her black hair was long and braided into two tails that reached the small of her back. She had a rather stuck-up, high-and-mighty look on her face. There was also more than a hint of annoyance when she recognized Ricky. Though Angela could certainly see them through Judy's shirt, the girl's breasts didn't look all that large to her. But she was no expert, of course.

"Judy," Ricky called again. "Yo, Judy, how you doing?!"

The girl's response was the kind of one-word dismissal that hurt more than a smack to the face. "Alright." That was all. After that, she turned away, talking with the older boys once again.

"Guess she's too good for me now," Ricky said more to himself than to Angela.

They inched ever closer to a foreboding cabin on the edge of the dense woods. To Angela, it seemed to loom large, stretching to the sky like an old house in a ghost story. Even before Ricky confirmed it, she knew that this was her bunk. This is where she would be abandoned. She would be dropped off at this rickety haunted house all alone. It didn't matter how many other girls were there with her, she would be by herself. None of those other girls were like her.

She looked at her cousin. Ricky knew this. Knew how hard it would be for her. And yet he fought for her to come to camp this year. He wanted her here. Didn't he know how difficult this was for her? Didn't he understand?

No. It was clear that he didn't. He was just a boy. A boy distracted by girls—girls with boobs!—and by the wild promise of the woods and the lake. Nature, in all its savage glory.

"This is it," he said as they reached the stoop of the haunted house. "If you need anything, I'll be in Bunk 19, below. Second from the bottom."

He lingered for a moment, not knowing what to do. Shuffling his feet, he approached her, looking down. A quick hug, a little pat on the back, and a kiss on the cheek. That was all she got in exchange for the impending horror.

Ricky left, heading vaguely down the hill, but tending towards the direction of Judy. A part of Angela left with him. She watched him go. There were no tears, but she was sad. Sad and scared.

That was when a voice spoke up in her head.

It was a strange voice but not unfamiliar. She had heard it before but only in the dead of night when she awoke from a bad dream. It was a scary voice but a curiously comforting one. A strong voice.

You don't need him, it said. *You don't need anyone.*

This was the voice of the Other Angela.

She would hear it many more times over the summer.

4

After Ricky left Angela he did track down Judy. In truth, he couldn't get away from his cousin fast enough. He loved her, of course, and was glad that she was finally here at camp this year, but he longed for the company of his friends and perhaps the warm, soft embrace of an attractive girl.

He had been hoping that this theoretical girl would be Judy, but he was no longer sure of this. So getting away from Angela was essential. He had to get to Judy, quickly, and see what was going on with her.

He caught up with her with ease. She had left the group of older, taller boys and was heading back to her bunk, towards him. When she saw him coming towards her, she sighed, making no effort to conceal her annoyance.

"Hey, who were all those guys?" Ricky asked when he reached her. He figured that it was best to be direct, to the point.

She shrugged. "Just some boys I met today."

Today? She had met them today?! His mind reeled. She had been here, what, less than fifteen minutes, and she was already meeting a gaggle of boys? It beggared belief. Ricky was lucky if he was going to meet any new girls the whole time he was at camp. That's why he was so looking forward to seeing Judy again. He already knew her, already had a relationship—of a kind, at least—with her. But looking at her now he could see that she had no interest in him any longer. She was maturing, developing, and older boys would now be taking an interest in her.

Ricky shook his head, let some of his inner thoughts tumble out. "Aren't they a little old for you?"

She shrugged. "Girls mature faster than boys do."

"That's bullshit and you know it!"

It just came out of his mouth, unbidden. In fact, he was certain that he had heard this before and suspected it was true, but there was no way he was going to let her get away with this. Not at the moment.

"I don't have time for any of your silly nonsense, Ricky," Judy said. That use of his name—flat, final. She was already walking away from him, discarding him like a piece of trash.

Ricky watched her go, staying where he was. For a moment, he could say nothing—his mind was a blank—and when a comeback finally did surface, Judy was too far away to hear it.

"Well excuse me," he said, thinking of some old sitcom, probably. Giving it a little bit more bite, he added, "Bitch." But it did no good. Judy was gone.

He feared that she would be gone the whole summer.

5

Susie had been working at Camp Arawak for enough summers now to recognize most of the girls. She nodded and greeted them as they filed into the cabin. Susie was a plain but pretty young woman in her twenties. The tips of her dark brown hair just tickled her shoulders. She wore the standard camp duds: white camp shirt with blue shorts.

Once all the girls were in the cabin—everyone waiting for Meg to arrive—Susie took a head count. There were only three new girls by her reckoning. Two of them appeared to be sisters, a pair of giggling blonde girls. The third was a quiet girl with black hair that kept to herself. The girl was already sitting on her bunk, staring off into the middle distance. There was something about her—something off. Susie couldn't quite put her finger on it.

Not everyone is comfortable at a place like this, she thought. *Give the girl some slack. She may need a little more help than the others. Probably just needs to come out of her shell.*

Susie looked about the cabin. Where the hell was Meg, anyway?

Figuring that she better go and check, she told the assembled girls to wait and performed a brief search. Finding the bathroom door closed, she rapped a quick knock on the door before opening it. Finding it unlocked, she went inside.

Meg, whose head was leaning over the sink, stiffened up and rubbed her nose, sniffing.

Her nostrils were red and her eyes weren't much better, though they were big and wide.

Susie frowned, disapprovingly. While it wasn't her place to tell another adult what she could or couldn't do, she found it distasteful to do drugs around a bunch of kids. She didn't say anything, though, and Meg didn't say anything, either. They only looked at each other for a brief moment as Meg sniffed and rubbed her nose once again.

She was an attractive young woman about the same age as Susie. Her dark hair was tied back in a severe knot. To Susie, it looked like a coiled snake. Despite the fact that it was tied back, she couldn't help but think of Medusa or one of the other gorgons. Stifling a laugh, Susie finally spoke. "You ready?"

Meg smiled and laughed. Nodded. "Let's do this."

She clapped her hands together, full of energy, and filed out of the bathroom and into the cabin proper. The noise made more than one of the girls jump a little, and Meg smiled as she came into the room.

"Alright, ladies," she said, "let's hurry up and get unpacked so that we can get these trunks the hell out of here."

She scanned the girls like a drill sergeant who had found the troops wanting. Shook her head. "I see a couple new faces here. So, for the benefit of them—and maybe those of you who don't have enough brains to remember—my name is Meg. M—E—G. Got it?"

Susie had sat down on a bunk next to one of the girls. Now Meg gestured towards her. "This is Susie. Got any problems, this is the complaints department. Capisce?"

The complaints department? Susie thought. *Is that what I am? Gee, that's a new one. Haven't heard that before.*

The girls went about unpacking. Susie helped out. One of the girls had brought a whole trunk's worth of stuff with her. It was heavy and took some time to clean out and arrange on the cubicles and shelves above and between the beds.

By the time that Susie was done, most of the other girls had already begun to settle in, each of them making their own little nests in their beds and the surrounding area. There were no partitions or marks on the ground, but territories had certainly been established. Each girl had her own plot of land. Here, near the door, was the Land of Cynthia. Beyond that was the Realm of Teresa. Smaller territories dotted the space further. But these were all small countries when compared to the Kingdom of Judy, off in one corner of the room.

It wasn't that Judy had any more room than any of the other girls, it was that her influence—her mere *presence*—was felt throughout the cabin. All the other fiefdoms looked upon Judy with some degree of fear.

All except one.

The new girl, the shy, silent one with black hair sat on her bed staring at Judy. There was no fear in her gaze. Susie, in fact, had a hard time reading the look on the girl's face. Was it fascination? Envy? Attraction, maybe? Hatred? Could it have been hatred? Susie didn't know.

Judy was curling her hair and hadn't yet noticed the girl staring at her. Susie looked from Judy to the girl and opened her mouth—ready to say what, she didn't know—but Judy cut her off, finally having noticed the strange girl's attention.

"What are you looking at?" she said.

She had stopped curling, the expensive-looking device held in place at the end of a particularly stubborn curl just below eye level. Susie could almost hear the sizzle of the iron as it slowly singed the tips of each strand of hair.

"What, are you taking a mental picture?" Judy continued. "Quit it!"

Meg moved quicker than Susie, putting herself in between the two girls just as Judy put the curler aside and stood up from her bed. She shot daggers at the shy, staring girl as she spoke. "What's going on here, huh? Speak up."

Suddenly, the shy girl's name came to Susie. *Idiot! How could*

I have forgotten? She sat down on the bed next to the girl, put an arm around her shoulders. The girl jerked slightly, as if startled by Susie's touch.

"You must be Angela," Susie said, then turned to Meg. "Remember, Ronnie told us about her."

Meg and Judy stared at Angela. To Susie, the two of them looked like a single unit, a coalition formed to oppose whatever it was Angela represented. The No Angelas Club, apparently. Meg shook her head slowly, looked at Judy.

"Looks like we got a real winner here," she said.

Judy chuckled mirthlessly. "You ain't kidding."

They went about their business. Meg retired to the bathroom once again, no doubt to powder her nose. Judy avoided Angela, which was probably for the best. Susie spent some time with Angela, talking to the girl, but couldn't get a word out of her. She was like a robot, carrying out tasks while tuning out everything else—a horse with blinders on.

Susie went to bed that night unsatisfied, frustrated with her failure to make any headway with Angela. She had always prided herself with the easy way that she could get a nervous, sometimes even scared, girl to smile or laugh. But Angela was something else entirely.

It would take some time to crack that particular egg.

6

Boys can be a handful. They respond more to the actions of their peers than to the orders of an adult, especially if said adult isn't a family member. This was why Gene tried to think of himself more as a kid than as an adult. Though he was pushing thirty years old, he had a youthful energy that was infectious. Same with his smile. He wasn't tall, but he was in great shape. His dark hair was always neatly trimmed. He was always tan no matter the season. He had an easygoing way about him.

More than one of the girls went home from Camp Arawak with a crush on him. A few of the boys, as well. But most of them went home thinking of him not as an authority figure, but as a friend.

Gene was determined to make this year the best year yet for the camp. His superiors, Ronnie and Mel, may not always be the best when it came to morale but, as far as he was concerned, that was why Gene was here.

Even on the first day, he had already created a camaraderie with the boys assigned to his cabin. As everyone was leaving for dinner that first night—boys shuffling out in their messy, uncoordinated yet somehow still graceful way—Gene heard raised voices coming from somewhere near the back of the cabin. He headed in that direction and saw two boys near the bathroom who looked ready to trade blows. One of them Gene recognized right away—Ricky Thomas, who Gene had known for several summers now—the other it took him longer to place. Finally he came up with a name, Trent, as he neared the boys.

"Take that back!" Ricky yelled.

"What's the matter with you?" Trent said, his eyes wide and stunned.

Before Gene could get to the two boys, Ricky grabbed Trent by the shirt and pushed him up against the wall. There was a sharp thud as the boy was slammed into the hard wood.

"Whoah," Gene said and rushed over. He grabbed Ricky and pulled him off the other boy. "What's going on here?" Faintly, he was aware of a figure stepping into the cabin—an adult, not a kid—but he didn't have time to address them at the moment.

"Nothing," Ricky said.

Trent gestured at the other boy. "He got all crazy all of a sudden!"

"Did not!" Ricky shouted and made for Trent.

Gene held him back. Sighed. "Somebody better give me an explanation." It was as tough a voice as he was capable of, but there was still that air of niceness about him, that sense of friendship and camaraderie that he couldn't shake—didn't want to shake.

"He was talking about my cousin!" Ricky said, an accusing finger pointed in Trent's direction.

"All I said was that she seemed a little odd," Trent said, still dumbfounded. "I just wanted to know if there was anything wrong with her."

"There's nothing wrong with her!" Ricky said.

"Easy," Gene said. He turned to Ricky. "It's your cousin's first summer here, isn't it, Ricky?" Ricky nodded. Gene returned the nod and addressed Trent. "She's just shy and nervous, then. Nothing wrong with her."

"Yeah!" Ricky said.

Gene turned back to Ricky. "But you gotta calm down, my man. Chill out. Now both of you go grab dinner."

Trent seemed relieved to escape, and he darted out of the cabin. Ricky followed more slowly. His gaze was directed off into the middle distance, as if he was contemplating something vast and unknowable. Both boys brushed past Mel Kostic, cigar in hand.

"Bit of an altercation," Mel said.

Gene shrugged. "Boys will be boys."

"Right," Mel said. He gestured out the cabin door with his cigar. "That last boy. Name's Ricky, right?"

Gene nodded. "Ricky Thomas."

"Ever had any problems with him before?"

"No. Just regular kid stuff. Gets into trouble here and there. Nothing like that, though."

Mel looked worried but about what, Gene didn't know. As far he could tell, there wasn't

anything to be worried about. It was summer. It was Camp Arawak. Nothing could ruin this magical time and place.

As Gene left the cabin to head to the rec hall, his spirits were ever so slightly dampened when he saw that the sunlight was beginning to wain. The day was ending. But no matter. It would be up again tomorrow. He looked at the natural beauty all around and smiled anyway. Nothing bad could happen in this place.

Nothing at all.

CHAPTER
THREE

CAMPFIRE TALES

1

"Who's new to camp this year? Raise your hands," Meg said with a cruel smile.

Two cabins worth of girls and two cabins worth of boys were arranged around a large campfire not far from the lake. Embers danced into the air as a good amount of kids raised their hands. Angela wasn't going to raise her hand at first, but she caught Ricky's expecting look from across the circle and finally joined the other newbies. It was the second night of sleepaway camp.

Meg gave a satisfied nod. "Okay. Quite a few of you. That means you don't know about the Horned Serpent. I feel that it's my duty as a counselor to keep you informed. To warn you, even."

She leaned forward, as if being drawn into her own story. The flickering flames cast phantasmagoric shadows across her face as she continued. "See, the native tribes in this area knew about this lake. Knew it was cursed." She locked eyes with Angela through the flames. "They knew there was a monster here."

A few of the younger kids looked at each in worry while the older kids smiled with glee. Angela kept a straight face. She was silent as the grave. Meg's gaze faltered and she found another young girl to torment with her stare.

"The Horned Serpent has been here longer than people have been around," Meg continued. "It's big. Real big. I'm told that no one has ever seen both of its ends at the same time. Mostly, it's hidden under the water. Watching. Lurking."

Angela looked around at everyone else. She settled on two of the counselors, Susie and Marie. They were sitting next to each other, Marie looking tired and leaning on the other young woman. Susie looked amused.

"It's not just a big snake, though," Meg said. "It's a shape-shifter. It can look like a girl if it wants to. A girl in the water, luring people until they're close enough to be snatched by the beast."

A wood knot exploded in the campfire and several of the younger kids jumped in alarm. Nervous laughter followed. Meg allowed herself one laugh before continuing.

"This is how it happens," she said. "If you're out on the lake at night—in one of the boats—the water will be eerily still. Like there isn't anything living in there at all. But you'll sense that something's not right. The hairs on the back of your neck will stand up. And then," she let the moment hang in the air for several seconds, "they'll be a knock on the boat."

She rapped three times on the log she was sitting on. "As if something in the water—*under* the water—was knocking on the boat. And your instinct will be to look over the side of the boat, to see what it is. To see if it's someone who needs help. Someone who's drowning!"

She sat up straight, a finger in the air. "But don't do it. Don't you look. If you look, it has you. You'll see a helpless girl floating in the water. Struggling. You'll be compelled to reach out and lend her a hand, to help her into the boat. But when your hand finally touches something, it won't be human skin that you feel. It'll be the smooth, ridged hide of the Horned Serpent. And you'll be pulled under the water to be smothered and drowned."

"That's not true," one of the younger boys said.

Everyone looked at him. The boy's name was Clark something-or-other. Angela had seen him around today.

"Oh, but it is true," Meg answered. "I've seen it myself."

Clark tried to scoff, but his voice caught in his throat, and he choked the scoff down, swallowed and looked around at the others for some kind of reassurance. There was none to be found.

"It was my first year here," Meg said with a reflective smile. "I decided it would be a good idea to take a boat ride by myself." Locking eyes briefly with Angela once again. "At night. It was a gorgeous night. Full moon! I snuck out of my cabin and took a boat out onto the water. Once I had rowed out to the middle of the lake, I started to feel uneasy. I was freaked out, I'm not ashamed to admit. Then I heard it." She rapped on the log once again. "The knocking. Three knocks on the outside of my boat."

Meg paused for dramatic effect. "But I'd heard the story. My cabin counselor, an old pro—she told me about the Horned Serpent. So I knew that I couldn't look. I shut my eyes and held them tight. Ages seemed to pass. Finally I heard splashing and the boat rocked as something massive moved under me and departed." She sighed. "Now, I'll admit to something else. I had to look. Just as it was leaving, I had to see. So I opened my eyes. Maybe ten, fifteen feet away from the boat, I saw a huge shape surface briefly before descending into the depths. It was a snake. A massive snake!"

A younger girl uttered a startled cry. Everyone else was silent.

"Then it was gone," Meg said. "Down to the deeps." She looked off into the middle distance and was silent for a moment. "You know, no one knows how deep this lake is.

People have tried to measure it, but they've all failed. Some of them have even disappeared. Who knows what's down there?"

"*Raaarrr!*"

There was a loud roar from outside the campfire circle and at least half of the campers jumped in alarm. An older boy came laughing into view, the flames illuminating his face. His name was Mike. Angela had seen him at dinner.

Mike half-heartedly apologized for scaring everyone and took a seat next to Judy. Angela had noted that Judy didn't jump when Mike roared. Had she been in on the prank?

There was scattered laughter from the older kids. Meg stood up, clapped once. "All right, all right, we've had our fun. It's getting late. I want everyone back in their bunks in ten minutes, got it?"

Groans of disapproval rippled through the group. As she stood up and made ready to leave, Angela spotted a girl who looked maybe eleven who was obviously crying but trying to conceal it, to hold it in. She wondered how the girl would sleep tonight—if she would sleep at all. She looked around. How many of the other kids would be struggling with the same?

The walk back to the cabin seemed longer than usual. The shadows were deeper. Darker. Angela—internal, as always—mused over the campfire tale as she trudged to bed. It stayed with her long into the night, well past lights out. She wasn't scared of the story while it was being told, but now—when one was alone with her own thoughts—it didn't seem so outlandish. Indeed, it was almost plausible.

That night, in bed, Angela tossed and turned, unable to find rest. After an hour or so of this, a voice spoke up in her head. It was the voice of the Other Angela.

You shouldn't be afraid, the Other Angela said. *Campfire tales are only scary if you*
believe them. Leave that to the weak.

Angela frowned.

You're not weak, the Other Angela answered her unspoken question. *You're stronger than you know.*

Slowly, Angela smiled, closed her eyes and rolled onto her side. After that, sleep came easy.

2

On the third day of camp, as she had every morning, Angela got up far earlier than any of the other girls. She went into the large bathroom at the back of the cabin. Along one side of the bathroom were toilet stalls. Opposite was a shower stall. Opposite the entrance sat a row of sinks.

Showering at the same time as the other girls was out of the question, of course. The stall only had an opaque plastic curtain for privacy. It wasn't private enough to feel really safe.

She went about her daily routine in silence. In fact, she hadn't spoken to anyone at all during her entire time at camp so far. But inside? Inside was another matter. Inside, she was screaming.

As she showered, she noted that her body was starting to sprout more hair everyday. Under her arms, between her legs— her legs themselves, even. This might prove to be a problem moving forward, but Angela wasn't sure how to solve it without help.

Despite how strange Aunt Martha could be, Angela wished that she were here with her, at camp. She would know what to do. What products to buy. There was even talk of a possible operation that would help Angela to transition fully. That would be good.

When she got out of the shower, she dried off and did her hair in front of one of the sinks, looking at her own reflection in the mirror. She thought of Pinocchio. He wanted to be a real boy. All Angela wanted was to be a real girl. That didn't seem like too much to ask. Sometimes she wished that the Blue Fairy would descend from the heavens, enter her room through the window one night, wave a magic wand, and make Angela whole.

But that wasn't the world.

Angela might have still been young, but she didn't believe that such things were real. She didn't believe in the Tooth Fairy, or Santa Claus, so she was under no illusions that she could be magically transformed by the wave of a wand.

All this ran through Angela's mind as she brushed her hair in front of the mirror. She didn't realize how hard she was brushing and pain shot through her scalp as several strands of hair ripped out by the root.

Frowning, she looked at the brush like it was an exotic weapon of some kind. Her gaze drifted from the brush back to the mirror, head tilted as she contemplated her own reflection.

3

The next day, the rec hall was bustling with loud children. Breakfast was simple: flapjacks, juice, ribbons of fried-too-long bacon, and mountains of bland scrambled eggs. The kids devoured it all.

Ronnie sat across from Mel at a table along one wall of the spacious building, talking shop as Meg approached. She had that mischievous smirk that Ronnie was starting to dislike. In fact, if he were in charge, Meg wouldn't be a counselor here at the camp. But the fact was that he wasn't in charge, not by a long-shot—Mel was in charge. And Mel liked Meg.

She stood by the table. Mel's hand snaked around her waist. Ronnie couldn't help but stare. It wasn't uncommon for counselors to pair off into couples, and he supposed there wasn't any law against Mel and Meg becoming a couple, either, but it didn't sit well with him. Were they sleeping together? Had it gone that far? He didn't know.

Suddenly, he felt self-conscious and concentrated on eating his breakfast. He had skipped the bacon after taking a good, long look at it, and was just about done with his flap-jacks. As he finished them, he tried to tune out Mel and Meg as they spoke. Whatever was going on between them was their business and their business alone. He didn't enter into it at all.

Therefore, it took him a moment to realize that Meg was addressing him. Finishing one final bite of flapjack, Ronnie looked up at her, eyebrows raised, and said, "Excuse me?"

"I said there's something wrong with Angela," Meg said with a small, annoyed sigh.

"What's wrong with her?" Ronnie asked.

"She's not talking."

Ronnie shrugged. "Is that a problem?"

Another sigh from Meg. "She's not eating, either."

Ronnie nodded, wiped at his mouth with a napkin, and stood up. "Let's go talk to her."

As the two of them left Mel's table, the man in question's hand snapped out with surprising speed and slapped Meg's behind. She only smiled and tittered laughter as Ronnie tried to ignore them once again.

The two of them approached a long table of girls—Meg's assigned bunk of campers. At one end of it sat Angela. She was looking off into space as if either contemplating some philo-sophical quandary or slipping into catatonia. Ronnie narrowed his eyes. The girl certainly did look off.

"See what I mean," Meg said, gesturing at Angela's full plate. "She hasn't even touched it."

Ronnie got down on one knee like he was proposing to Angela, looked her in the eye. She looked blandly back at him—not catatonic, then. "Hi, Angela. I'm Ronnie, remember? Meg tells me you aren't eating much. That true?"

Meg crossed her arms and shook her head. "You won't get a peep out of this one."

Ronnie gave Meg a quick, dismissive glance before returning his attention to Angela. "Tell you what. Why don't we go in the kitchen and see if we can't get you something you'll like. How does that sound?"

He stood up and took hold of the girl's hand. She moved like a robot in a science fiction movie. "I'm gonna take her in the kitchen to see Artie," he said to Meg. "She'll be alright. Probably just a little homesick is all."

As they left, Ronnie heard Meg speak to the rest of the table, not bothering to whisper. "He's starting to spoil the little brat already."

Ronnie only shook his head and kept his mouth shut. It wouldn't do anyone any good to cause a scene right in the middle of breakfast. Often, when he had taken kids into the kitchen in the past, Ronnie had noted that they all looked around in wonder—their child's eyes never having seen a kitchen so large, never having seen so much food stockpiled in one place before. Like they had just walked onto Willy Wonka's factory floor. But not Angela. She looked straight ahead, like a horse with blinders on.

Ben was at the griddle, finishing off a few more rounds of scrambled eggs for the kids who were brave enough to ask for seconds. He smiled a welcome.

"Artie around?" Ronnie asked.

Before the older man could even answer, Artie himself emerged from the large walk-in pantry, a can of Schlitz beer in one hand, apron spattered with old stains. He looked unkempt-in-an-ordered-sort-of-way, a state of being that seemed unique to Artie and Artie alone. Ronnie frowned inwardly before speaking up. "Can you be a little more discreet with that stuff, Artie?" He gestured to the beer can.

"Sure," Artie said amiably enough and set the can aside. He smiled and looked down at Angela. "What's up?"

"I want you to meet one of our new campers. This is Angela. Angela, this is Artie, our head chef."

Artie leaned over, getting in Angela's face, his nose almost touching her nose. "Well, hello, Angela."

Ronnie frowned, but a phone ringing in the other room shook him out of his head and he looked past Artie. "Can you get that for me, please, Ben?"

"Of course," Ben said.

Ronnie frowned again. What had he been thinking about? He shook it off and returned to the matter at hand. "As you can see," he said, "Angela isn't all that talkative. She also isn't much of a fan of your cooking, either."

"Is that so?" Artie said with a smirk.

"Think you could find something for her. Maybe some ice cream, or maybe some—"

Ben poked his head back into the kitchen. "Phone call for you and Mel, Ron."

Ronnie turned to him. "OK, thanks, Ben. I'll grab it." He turned back to Artie. "Do me a favor. Find her something she likes."

"No problem," Artie said. "I'll take care of her."

Ronnie tried to let go of Angela's hand. She didn't seem to want him to leave. But he smiled and pulled away.

As he left, he heard Artie say, "I'll bet we can find something interesting in the walk-in. You never know what you can find in there."

For one more brief second, Ronnie considered forgetting about the phone call and returning to Angela.

"Ron?" Ben said, still in the doorway to the kitchen.

That snapped him out of it. What was he being so worried about? Nothing was going to happen to Angela. What could possibly be a danger to her here? She was with an adult.

She was perfectly fine.

4

Ricky didn't see Angela anywhere. She wasn't at her table. He walked over to Meg, who was just lounging in her chair, a superior look on her face. "You seen my cousin?"

Meg took a moment to let Ricky know that she wasn't happy to be speaking to him. "Ronnie took her into the kitchen."

"She eat anything?"

"What do you think?"

Ricky didn't answer. His mind was racing. The kitchen. Ronnie took Angela to the kitchen. That was where Artie was, the head chef. Ricky didn't like Artie. He was way too friendly with the kids, the girls especially. That pervert didn't deserve to be around any children, let alone his cousin.

"What's her problem, anyway?" Meg said, interrupting his thoughts. "She don't eat, she don't talk, she don't do anything."

"Why don't you leave her alone?" Ricky said. "She's just quiet."

"If she were any quieter, she'd be dead."

But Ricky was already off, on his way to the kitchen. He didn't intend to potentially leave his cousin alone with that creep.

5

As it happened, Angela *was* alone with Artie. The pantry was claustrophobic, trapped inside it with a man as big and imposing as Artie was, looming over her and leering. Angela watched a single bead of sweat dribble off the tip of his chin.

The shelves on either side were packed with food. Cans and cans of all manner of cheap goods, the kind of stuff kids loved. Angela wished she could crawl inside one of them and disappear.

"See anything you like?" Artie said. He gestured to the shelves with his big hands, his smile wide. When he lowered his arms, his hands settled on his hips, his fingertips just ever so slightly scratching at his bulging crotch.

"Maybe I can help you decide," the big man continued. The big hands fiddled with the big belt he was wearing. More sweat trailed down his face. "You sure are a sweet-looking little cupcake, ain't you?"

The shelves now seemed to be closing in on either side of them. Cans on the top shelf, high above, seemed to be tilting towards Angela, as if they were going to tip over the side and bury her. She had never felt more trapped.

Artie unbuckled his belt. The sound of metal on leather was deafening in this too-small space, and Angela clasped both hands to her head. She reached out for that other voice, the Other Angela, but heard nothing.

The big man was shaking, as if his actual flesh itself was sentient and wanted out of his restraining clothes. Drenched in sweat, his face red and twitching, lips glistening. He smelled like week-old roast beef.

Angela was frozen in place. Silently, she cried out for help, either from some savior in the flesh or that nebulous Other Angela.

"Yeah," Artie said, his voice breaking. "Think I got something you're gonna like real good."

"What are you doing?"

As Artie quickly buckled his pants and turned, Angela sighed in relief. Her prayers had been answered: Ricky was in the pantry with them now, a look of rage on his face.

Artie froze in utter disbelief—but the rage came quick enough. The big man grabbed hold of Ricky and picked him up by the shoulders. Slammed him against the wall. A can of creamed corn fell from the top shelf and glanced off Ricky's shoulder.

"You keep your mouth shut, you hear me?" Artie spit at the boy, their noses only an inch apart. "You didn't see nothin'!" Ricky struggled, defeated. "Got it?" Artie growled. "Nothin'!"

Ricky smirked, "Sure. Whatever you want."

Artie let go of the boy and he dropped to the floor "Now get the hell outta here!" A sweep of his large, meaty arm sent the two of them running from the pantry and to the relative safety of the kitchen.

6

Mel had just finished a stressful phone call with his creditors. He had handled it well and kept up a good front, but it had rattled him all the same. After it was over, he lit up another cheap cigar and headed into the kitchen. What he really wanted was a drink, but he was trying to cut back. Plus, it was still technically breakfast time, and Mel liked to think he had class.

He entered the kitchen just in time to see Angela and Ricky come running out of the walk-in pantry. They rushed by Mel and out into the main area of the rec hall. Ricky's face was a mask of barely-concealed rage. Mel narrowed his eyes.

Coming out of the walk-in just behind them was Artie. The head chef looked flustered, but he also had an air of nonchalance about him as he went back to manning the griddle.

"What was that all about?" Mel asked, taking his cigar from between his lips and gesturing to the door where the two children had disappeared.

Artie shrugged and avoided Mel's eyes. "Guess I must have scared 'em."

That was all. He went back to the griddle, as if saying, "Look, I got work to do here. Never you mind."

Mel didn't like to be dismissed, but he had more important things to worry about. More important things like whether he would be able to keep the camp open another summer. The numbers weren't looking good.

Mel puffed away at his cigar and wandered out of the kitchen. Hanging near the entryway was a strip of flypaper. It was yellow, crusted, full of insects dying and dead. It didn't smell—or, at least, Mel couldn't smell it over the cigar smoke—but it was disgusting all the same. The camp owner made a mental note to ask his staff to, at the very least, take it down and replace it with a new one. This mental note went no further than that.

7

That evening, while cooking dinner for the ravenous brats, Artie couldn't shake the feeling that he was being watched.

But aside from Ben, who was sitting in the corner peeling potatoes, Artie was alone. A large pot of corn boiled on the stove top. This wasn't exactly regulation—Mel had made it clear that it was a danger to have that much boiling water on the stove top—but what the camp owner didn't know wouldn't hurt him. Besides, it was a lot quicker to cook it this way.

Artie poured more salt into the pot—a generous portion—and stirred the concoction. He smiled at the way the ears of corn swirled around the pot. They were like little people that he was boiling alive.

Small things that he could control—that's what Artie liked. Little things, like little people, that were easy to control if you knew what you were doing. He frowned. The corn needed more salt. According to Artie's method of cooking, everything needed more salt. Sadly, the shaker was empty.

"Gonna grab some hay before dinner," Ben said. "You comin'?"

Distracted, Artie said, "Yeah, after I find some more goddamn salt."

Ben chuckled as he got up from his chair, then he was out the door and gone.

Artie knew that there was more salt in the walk-in pantry, but he was too lazy to go grab it. There was another big can of the stuff somewhere here in the kitchen. Where was it? He scratched his chin, looked around. There it was. Way up on the top shelf above the stove.

"Son of a bitch," he said, and turned to grab a chair. For just a moment that sense of being watched returned. The hairs on the back of his neck stood up. A quick look behind told him that there was no one there.

Paranoia was a natural state for Artie. He had to be paranoid considering the kind of company he liked to keep, the kind of people he was attracted to. He had to keep on his toes—

had to have eyes in the back of his head.

He mounted the chair and stood on it. Of course it wobbled. Why wouldn't it? And of course the salt was still just out of reach. And was that the patter of small feet rushing across the kitchen floor towards him? He half-turned, but he was too late: someone grabbed hold of his chair legs and yanked.

Artie reached out for something, finding the edges of the large—boiling, steaming—stove pot. He screamed in scalding pain and made to let go of the pot—*stopped.*

He couldn't let go. *Hands steamed, skin melted.* If he did so, he would fall to the floor and the pot would tip over onto him. He was precariously balanced on the chair, which stood on only two legs in front of the stove.

The person—the *child*—was still there, still had hold of the chair he was barely standing on. His hands sizzled. "Hey, kid, what the fuck are you doing back there? Let me down now!"

Frantically, he turned his head but still couldn't make them out, whoever they were. He could feel the flesh of his hands slide off the muscle. "Help! Jesus Christ, somebody help me! Ben! Ben!"

The child yanked once again. Artie tried to catch himself on the edge of the stove, calling out one final time—"BEN!" His hands, burned and useless now, succeeded in tipping the large pot over as he crashed to the ground, landing on his back, screaming as boiling hot water splashed over him.

The splash of liquid death filled his eye sockets, his nose, his mouth, with wet fire. Artie's screams turned to gurgles. It was the worst pain he had ever experienced in his entire miserable life.

His tongue melted away, leaving an open, silent, red maw in

its place. His eyes followed soon after. The world above him went white and brilliant, then completely black. His nostrils burned from the inside and he smelled a mixture of boiled corn and scalded flesh before he lost his scent entirely. Consumed by blind, piercing agony, he could hear everything. His ears had never been more acute, more precise, than in these last, horrible moments.

The pot that he had tipped over, still rolling—spinning in place. The child who had done this to him running from the kitchen at the exact same moment that someone—presumably Ben—rushed in.

Worst of all he could hear the large salt shaker on the stove above him, spinning slowly and coming to a stop at the shelf's edge, top completely off. Salt poured over on him like a storm, acid on his burns. Filling his mouth. Suffocating.

Pain. Shame and anger. Shame at how he had lived his life, and anger that it was ending all the same. And rage that Ben was still standing there in the outer doorway of the kitchen, not moving. Not helping. Was it shock? Or was it something else that held him back?

Artie didn't know and, as salt filled his lungs, he didn't care. He was dying. His body convulsed. Boiling water liquified his eyes, seeped through his skull to get to his brain.

One more desperate gasp inhaled a lungful of salt, Artie's legs kicked out, he pissed and shit himself, and died.

No one mourned him.

CHAPTER
FOUR

SUMMER GAMES

1

Ben simply *knew* what Mel was going to do even before he did it. It was written all over the nervous camp owner's face. Even as he chomped on that cigar—a mask like any other, Ben thought—it was clear to see that Mel was thinking about the exposure, the way that this accident—*and it had to be an accident, had to be*—could negatively affect the camp.

Ben and Mel conferred with the doctor in the kitchen, the rest of the kitchen staff a respectful distance back. They had called an ambulance even though it was clear that Artie was already—mercifully—dead. It just seemed like the thing to do. Back when Ben was a kid, his family would call them meat wagons. In his neighborhood, in Harlem, ambulances would always arrive too late—the victim already dead and gone. All they did was collect the meat. That was what was on his mind now. Artie was nothing more than meat.

He hadn't liked the man, but he had been someone to talk to. It wasn't his loss that was troubling Ben, it was the suddenness of his death. It was an accident—*had to be*. Despite what Ben had seen, it was just an accident. Artie had stood on a chair to grab some salt on a high shelf, slipped and fell, taking the pot with him. That was all.

"Doc," Mel said, grabbing the cigar from his mouth and gesturing with it, "think he died quick?" A flick of the cigar at the spot where Artie had fallen.

The doctor—Ben didn't know his name—sighed, eyes going wide as he thought about it. Shook his head. "I hope so. It was certainly quick in a literal sense, but it probably seemed like ages to him, I'm afraid to say."

Mel nodded, quiet for a moment. The men from the meat wagon had already taken Artie's body out of the kitchen. They had covered it in a sheet before wheeling it into the van.

"And it was just an accident," Mel said, making the prayer a statement.

The doctor shrugged. "Seems to be, but I'm no investigator. I'm not sure about those

burns on his hands."

"Need anything else from us?" By *us*, Mel meant himself. Ben could tell from the man's face that he had no intention of letting any of the rest of them, Ben included, talk to the doctor. "I'd like to move this thing along. No need to upset the campers, right?"

"No," the doctor said, "I guess I'll be on my way."

Mel nodded. Ben could tell that the man was cooking something up. And whatever it was, it couldn't be good. "What now?" Ben asked.

"Now," Mel said with a sigh, "we get this ambulance the hell out of here as quick as we can, before anyone else sees it." Ben narrowed his eyes. "Hey," Mel said, "it was just an accident! No need to upset any of the kids or their parents, am I right?"

"I guess so." He looked past Mel to the small kitchen staff in the corner. Flies buzzed around in the air between the two groups. Ben nodded to the small group. "What about them?"

"I'll take care of them." He smirked—actually *smirked*—and

went over to the kitchen staff, hand disappearing into a pocket and coming out with a modest stack of bills. "Real shame what happened to Artie. People need to be more careful around here." He began to count out the bills. "Dangerous place." Began to dole them out to each young man. "You all be careful in here. Understand?" There were nods all around.

Mel gave them a smile and returned to Ben, swatting away a fly or two. "Ben," he said, "I don't think it's a good idea to tell anyone about what happened here. If anyone asks, Artie took a tumble, he's getting it looked at, and he won't be back the rest of the summer. Got it?"

Ben cocked his head to one side and, in that moment, considered telling Mel what he had seen when he burst into the kitchen right after Artie had taken that tumble. Considered it but decided against it. What he said was, "Well, I don't know."

Mel frowned but in a sympathetic way. Put a hand on Ben's shoulder. "Listen. You're head man around here now, right?"

Ben nodded. "Right."

"And we still gotta a lotta hungry mouths to feed, right?"

"Right."

"Besides," that smirk again, "an extra fifty bucks more a week can't be all that bad, can it?"

"No, sir," Ben said right away. He was starting to come around to Mel's plan already.

That was the way it worked. Mel had bad ideas, but they were bad ideas that made sense in a twisted sort of way. And it wasn't as if Ben was going to miss Artie. He knew what the man got up to on his off hours. And now that he was gone? Who really cared? In fact, it was a weight off Ben's shoulders. No one would miss him around here.

Mel turned to regard the young kitchen staff. "And fifteen dollars a week more for the rest of you, eh?"

"Thanks, sir," one of them piped up. Ben couldn't remember the boy's name.

Mel leaned back to Ben. "Make sure our friends here are on

the same page as the two of us. No need to let any gruesome details out. Understand?"

"You don't have to worry none about them," Ben said.

"Good, good. I knew I could count on you. What do you say we get dinner back up and running again, huh?"

"Right away, sir."

Mel gave Ben another pat on the shoulder and stuck his cigar back in his mouth. Chomped on it. Left through the open door leading outside. The same door that they had wheeled out Artie's body to the meat wagon. Ben watched Mel leave, and leaned against the doorframe. The meat wagon was gone now. Ben didn't see any kids milling around, so maybe they had gotten away with it. Who knew?

Ben rubbed the old doorframe and looked off into the middle distance. There was one kid who knew, of course. When he ran into the kitchen after Artie took his tumble, Ben had seen a child running from the kitchen into the rec hall. The horrible look on the child's face had told Ben everything he needed to know. But that wasn't the worst part.

The worst part was that Ben had recognized the child.

2

Mozart was looking at Paul's ass crack, a cheek touching either side of his nose. This was not a sight which he was particularly interested in seeing in the middle of a fine, summer day.

The circumstances which led to Mozart's face connecting with Paul's ass were incredibly

stupid. Or so they seemed in retrospect. While they were happening, everything seemed entirely plausible.

Mozart was a bit of a nerd. He wore glasses and always seemed to have a nosebleed. His real name wasn't Mozart, of course. His name was Robert, but he had been interested in music when he was little and one of the older boys in his school had started calling him Mozart and it had stuck. He didn't exactly like it, but he wasn't the kind of person to argue something like this, either.

Today, he was in his cabin with the other boys. They were all killing time until the game started. Mozart didn't really like baseball, but he enjoyed spending time with the other boys, enjoyed being outside, even if he would rather be playing games of the more handheld, video variety. He planned to squirrel one away in his back pocket, bringing it with him to the game. Baseball could get boring sometimes.

They had all been at sleepaway camp for a week now. Mozart had been having a good time. He had heard some talk— rumors were all they were—about something happening to the head chef, Artie, but he didn't believe them. It was true that Artie was no longer anywhere to be found, but it was more likely that he just skipped out of his job early. Maybe he got a better offer somewhere. Whatever the explanation, the food was better now anyway.

Ricky suggested that a bit of mind-over-matter was called for. A demonstration. He claimed that through some mild hypnosis, he could make any physical action impossible. A single sit-up, for example. And Mozart, being the one most skeptical, was chosen as the group volunteer.

He told Mozart to lay down on the floor, eyes closed, and listen to his voice. Ricky would convince Mozart's mind to deny his muscles the ability to move.

"One single sit-up," Ricky said, drawing out each word. "You won't even be able to perform that simple act."

"There's no way," Mozart had said.

"Be quiet and concentrate."

So Mozart had sighed and concentrated on Ricky's voice. There was no way this was going to work—he knew that—but he was intrigued, all the same. What if Ricky was telling the truth? So when Ricky told him to try a sit-up, Mozart did.

And his face smacked right in the crack of Paul's ass. The boy squatted over him, shorts pulled down, ass in his face. It had not been pretty, at least not to Mozart. "You guys are gross!" he said to a chorus of laughter.

Paul pulled up his underwear and shorts and let Mozart get up. As he did, the outside door to the cabin opened and Gene came in. He took a quick look at the proceedings, smiled to himself, tried to stifle a chuckle and failed. "Don't tell me Mozart fell for the old mind-over-matter trick."

"Oh, not Mozart," Ricky said. "He's too clever. Am I right?"

Mozart just shot the other boy a shit-eating grin as another rumble of laughter echoed through the cabin. Gene quieted everyone down with raised hands. "All right, everybody got your gear together?"

At least half of the boys shouted out, "Yes!" It was finally time for the game. Their cabin had challenged one of the other cabins to a baseball game. As Mozart grabbed his gear, he sighed. They were going to lose. Any team that he was on always lost. He was starting to wonder if he just had terrible luck or something. What made it worse today was that the other cabin was composed of older boys. They were bigger and meaner. What chance did Mozart and his bunk mates have?

The game had been Ricky's idea, of course, and he had been backed up by Paul. Ricky had something against one or two of the older boys. Mozart didn't know what it was, and he didn't want to know—all he knew was that now the whole cabin had become involved in whatever it was.

"Great," Gene said, clapping his hands together, "everybody ready?"

"More than ready," Ricky answered for everyone.

"Good, cause I got five bucks riding on you all to win this thing."

"Is that allowed?" Mozart asked. He was genuinely curious.

Gene shrugged. "Who can say?"

There was some laughter as Mozart frowned, trying to

figure out what Gene meant. Was he making some kind of joke —maybe one at Mozart's expense?

Mozart thought about it all the way to the baseball field. He often felt left behind in matters like this. Always the brunt of the joke, never the puller of them.

When everyone got to the pitch, Mozart found a spot in the outfield—way out in the

outfield—and tried to stay out of everyone's way. Maybe he could get some time on his video game when things got slow.

3

Ricky looked at Bill across the plate with real hatred. The fucker was just so *smug*. Even now, when his team was down by a run, Bill still looked smug. It was as if he knew something that Ricky didn't.

Bill was one of the older boys that Judy had been talking to on the first day of camp. They thought they were such hot shit. Ricky shook his head. He'd show them.

Where the hell was Mike, anyway? Ricky looked around and found the older prick hanging out just past the dugout, talking to some younger girl that Ricky didn't recognize. As long as it wasn't Judy that the big bastard was talking to.

"What's the holdup, pencil dick?" Bill said from the plate.

"Just thinking about screwing your sister," Ricky said.

"Big talk from somebody that's gonna lose big today."

"You're down a run. You're the one that's gonna lose big time."

"We'll see. You and your little babies wanna make a little wager while the game's still close or are you too chicken shit?"

"What'd you have in mind, asswipe?"

"Buck a man, asshole!"

"That's a little steep." Ricky pretended to consider it. Slapped the bat into his free hand a few times. "Make it five."

"You're on, fucker!"

Ricky smiled and hit a hard grounder straight past the smug son of a bitch. He made it to second base with ease.

The game went pretty smoothly after that. The bigger boys got two more runs but Ricky and his teammates matched them, keeping their lead. There was a hairy moment when it looked like Mozart was going to miss an easy catch—*was the little nerd actually playing his handheld video game?*—but he caught it at the last minute, sending Mike back to the dugout to talk to his increasingly-less-interested lady hangers on.

When Ricky's team was up 8-6, he and Bill faced each other over the plate once again, their positions reversed. Bill behind the plate, Ricky at the pitcher's mound.

"Strike him out, Ricky!" Gene shouted from the sidelines.

"No problem, Geno," Ricky said with the confidence of a much older player, "this guy blows dead dogs."

"Eat shit and die, Ricky!" Bill said, pointing his bat across the plate. That pointed use of his first name. Ricky hated hearing it come out of the smug bastard's mouth.

"Eat shit and live, *Bill!*"

Ricky zipped the ball right past the mouthy bastard.

"Strike!"

The big, smug bastard was so pissed off he couldn't hit for shit. Ricky struck him out no problem at all. The game was locked up. Ricky's victory, when it came, was almost anti-climactic. They celebrated it just the same.

Even Mozart, who had zero interest in outdoor sports, was excited. Probably because now they were all a little bit richer.

4

It was a day after the big baseball game—everyone in camp had heard about it by now—and now all of the girls and some of the younger boys were at the archery range. Marie stood off to one side of the targets, arms folded across her chest, monitoring the whole range. Angela took careful aim with the bow, one eye closed, the tip of her tongue poking out of her mouth. Susie stood behind Angela, watching the girl's progress.

It had been hard, Susie didn't mind admitting to herself. Angela was a tough egg to crack. She still hadn't spoken to anyone in days. Only following orders, nodding "yes" or shaking her head "no." At least she was eating. That was progress, Susie supposed.

"Bet she can't even hit the ground near the target!" one of the younger boys said. Susie gave him a disapproving look. The boy, Bobby, screwed up his face and smirked, as if to say, "You're not *my* counselor."

Susie just sighed and turned her attention back to Angela. The girl looked discouraged, eyes cast down. Susie took a chance and gently grabbed hold of both of the girl's shoulders from behind. Gave her a pat. "You can do it."

Angela didn't smile, but it was clear that she appreciated Susie's encouragement. The girl raised the bow and took aim once again.

"Creepy Angela!" one of the other boys, Clark, called out, hands cupped around his mouth to project the sound of his voice. "Creepy, creepy Angela can't shoot straight!" Bobby laughed beside him.

Susie turned away from Angela and approached the boys. There were three of them, Bobby, Clark, and a weaselly little brat named George. She bent over to look them in the face.

"Stop that," she said. "You have no right to pick on Angela. She hasn't done anything to you."

The boys only smiled and tried to contain their laughter. George covered his mouth with both hands.

"If Angela weren't a better person," Susie continued, "she might make you regret that! She's much bigger than you."

More laughter from the boys.

"Just think about that!" Susie said.

There was a *thunk* as an arrow hit the hay target. All three of the boys looked past Susie, stunned. Susie followed the direction the arrow would have flown and found it sticking in the target, dead center.

Susie saw that Marie was just as stunned as she was. Leaving the boys where they stood, Susie crossed the distance between herself and Angela. The girl had no expression on her face at all. A total blank. It was intimidating. Susie stood next to her, not knowing what to say right away. Finally, she shook her head and said, "Great job, Angela."

Angela just looked up at her impassively. Anything could be going on behind those eyes. Susie was able to maintain her smile, but there was something about that blank expression.

Something she didn't trust.

5

The rec hall was a shithole.

There wasn't any other word for it—the place was an absolute shithole. Judy had never liked it, but it was where everyone was most nights at Camp Arawak, so that's where Judy was tonight. She and Meg had been dishing, about boys, about camp, about the absolute state of the rec hall—the walls were covered in graffiti, how could anyone *stand* it?—but Meg had left after Mel had entered, and now Judy was alone.

She had suspected it before, but now she was convinced that Meg was dating Mel, or at least, she was interested in the camp owner. Judy shook her head as she watched the two of them talking across the hall. It was gross. The old man must have been sixty. What was Meg thinking?

Judy scanned the rec hall, looking for something interesting. Despite what she thought, she wasn't, strictly speaking, alone. There was a small group of guys hanging around near her, trying to get her attention, but she paid them no mind. Three of the older boys, Mike, Billy, and Kenny, looked like they were plotting something. She could hear what they were saying.

"We still need some more babes," Bill said.

Babes. Why hadn't they asked her? She was the prettiest one here by far. It made absolutely no sense that they hadn't asked her yet.

"I mean," Kenny said, "who wants to go skinny dipping with fifteen guys and only five girls?"

Judy raised one eyebrow like Mr. Spock. *She* certainly wanted to go skinny dipping with fifteen guys. Bill looked around the rec hall and Judy looked away, trying to act natural, trying to look sexy, trying to be the one to get picked. She thought about what she would say to them. Should she play hard to get? Should she refuse, then show up later anyway?

"Hey, let's ask Angela," Bill said.

Judy immediately looked back at the small group, then across the room to where Angela was sitting by herself eating a candy bar. How could the boys possibly want Angela to skinny dip with them and not her? How stupid were they?

"Man," Kenny said, "I've been watching her all week and she is fucked up."

Exactly, Judy thought. Kenny still had his wits about him, it seemed.

"Now, wait a minute," Mike said. "You guys aren't afraid to ask Angela, are you? I think it might be interesting if Angela were around tonight."

Judy looked on disapprovingly. Mike was the oldest non-counselor here and he wanted to skinny dip with Angela, an actual child, and not her? The bastard.

"Then you go ask her," Bill said.

"Oh, I would, I would," Mike said, "but it wasn't my idea. Who am I to steal a buddy's great idea, huh? Unless, of course, you're both chicken?" And then he actually made squawking noises, folded his arms and flapped them like wings. He was so childish, like all boys, it seemed.

Bill shook his head and walked away, hands raised. He was out. Mike looked at Kenny.

"Alright," Kenny said, "I'll do it! Who knows? We may get married one day."

Kenny started across the rec hall towards Angela, followed by Mike. Angela finished her candy bar, crumpled up the wrapper and tossed it deftly into a trash can a few feet away.

"Nice shot," Mike said as the two boys approached.

Angela looked towards them, frozen like a deer in headlights. She made no move to leave—no move at all—and just sat there imitating a statue.

"Hey, Angela," Kenny said, looking down for a moment—Jesus, he was actually blushing—before seeming to regain some confidence. "We're all going down to the lake tonight. You know, for a little swim. And, um, we were kind of wondering if, well, maybe if you wanted to join us or something."

No answer. Angela remained silent, like she had been the entire time she had been at camp. For a brief moment, Judy found herself siding with Angela. If Kenny had approached her with this lame attempt then he deserved the silent treatment.

"Let the pro take over," Mike said, pushing Kenny aside and taking center stage. He was all swagger and forced charm. "What say me and you go for a little walk somewhere, talk about tonight, huh?"

This would have worked on Judy, but it had no effect on Angela. The girl remained just as immobile as ever. Judy raised both eyebrows. Angela was a cold one, that was for sure.

Across the hall, Kenny shook his head, getting visibly frustrated. He turned away from Angela to face Mike. "See, I told you she was playing with half a deck. She's nutty as a fruit cake." Turned back to Angela. "Ain't that right, Angela? Ain't you Looney Tunes?"

The main door of the rec hall opened and Ricky and Paul sauntered in like they were tough shit. Judy looked at the two of them with contempt. She had enjoyed Ricky's company the previous summer, but she had grown since then while he had stayed an angry little boy. Now, walking into the rec hall, he wore a ridiculous cowboy hat on his head, a white feather—*for cowards*, Judy chuckled to herself—sticking out of the brim. She had heard about the baseball game, of course. Apparently, Ricky and his friends thought that winning a stupid game made them cock of the walk or something.

She shook her head and turned her attention back to Kenny, Mike, and Angela. Mike stood stiff as a board, eyes fixed in place. He was doing a pretty good impression of Angela and Judy had to stifle a laugh.

"How's this?" Mike said to Angela. "Remind you of anyone you know?"

Kenny chuckled, then added his two cents. "Yo, Angela. How come you're so fucked up? I mean, like, what's your problem?"

Judy looked at Ricky and Paul to make sure they had noticed what was going on. If they hadn't, Judy fully intended to tell them. But there was no need. Ricky was already in motion, rushing across the rec hall to protect the dignity of his cousin.

This oughta be good, Judy thought.

"Hey, dickface," Ricky shouted at Kenny, "leave her alone!"

Everyone in the rec hall watched them. Judy saw Mel take a step towards the altercation, but he didn't make a move to stop anything. *Good*.

"Oh yeah?" Kenny said. "What are you gonna do about it, asshole?"

Ricky made the first move, surging towards Kenny and throwing a punch at the bigger boy. He missed by a mile and Kenny countered with a good shot into the younger boy's stomach. Ricky folded over, but he wasn't down long. He came up with a punch to Kenny's jaw, snapping the older boy's head back. Kenny rebounded with a fury, landing a strike across Ricky's nose.

Ricky tumbled over onto his back and Kenny launched himself on top of him. Mike got involved, too, getting ready to defend his friend. Paul entered into the fray at the same moment. Soon, several punches were being thrown by at least five boys. Judy was getting excited. She crossed her legs and smiled to herself as the boys fought.

It didn't last long. Gene shouted for everyone to quit it and started pulling boys off the pile. Susie stood behind him, looking worried, but ready to help if she could. The two of them

were no fun at all. Mel watched from a safe distance back.

Gene grabbed Ricky off the ground and had to hold him back. Ricky tried to launch himself at Kenny and Mike once again. He shot an accusing finger at them.

"You fucks!" he screamed, his voice breaking. "I'm gonna beat your fucking asses in!"

"You and what army?" Kenny said.

Gene shook his head. "Shut up and let's go." He gestured with his hand, ushering Kenny, Mike, Bill and a few of the others out of the rec hall. They reluctantly left.

"Pricks!" Ricky yelled after them as they left.

Gene slapped the back of Ricky's head. "Shut your mouth, will you? Mel's watching."

"I don't give a shit," Ricky said.

"I think I'd better take you over to the infirmary before your mouth gets you into any more trouble."

The two of them left the rec hall together. Judy, still smiling, still turned on by the whole thing, looked about, settling on Paul, who was still here. She thought about getting up and talking to him. The boy had never really done anything for her before, but the way he had launched into the fray to help his friend was pretty exciting.

Before she could make a move, Paul headed over to Angela and sat down beside her. *What the fuck?* Judy thought. *Why is everyone interested in stupid little Angela?*

"Hi," Paul said to Angela. "I'm Paul. Ricky's friend. You remember?"

She nodded. And was that a smile beginning to play around the edges of her lips? It fucking *was*. The bitch.

"Listen," Paul continued. "I heard… Well, I mean, Ricky told me about what happened to you when you were little. Well anyway, I'm really sorry about your family."

Angela nodded again, looking sad as a memory seemed to cross her mind. Judy narrowed her eyes. What had happened to the girl? And whatever it was, was it why she was so fucked up now? What could it have been?

"Me and Ricky go back a long way," Paul said. "Three years already." He looked towards the main door where Ricky had left with Geno. "We always seem to get into trouble." Smiled when he turned his attention back to Angela. "Last year we hung a bunch of the girls' panties on the flagpole."

There was that smile threatening to cross Angela's face. Whatever Paul was doing was

working. Judy felt her face flush with rage.

"Sorry," Paul said, as if he might have offended her. Couldn't he see her face? What was he, stupid or something? "We got caught anyway. Last year, we locked Alan Weinstein out of the cabin with no clothes on. Man, did we get in trouble for that one."

That smile again. And perhaps the beginnings of a laugh—a chuckle, at least. Angela was actually *charmed* by the boy. It made Judy want to puke. It made her want to rip every strand of Angela's hair out of her head.

"Bunk 19, time to go," Gene said, reappearing at the door. He gestured to his boys, ushering them out. "Say your good-byes and let's go."

"Well," Paul said with a sigh, "guess I gotta go. Good night."

He got up and started towards Gene. Then a miracle happened. Angela *spoke*.

"Good night," she said. Her voice was hesitant, and a little deeper than Judy had imagined it, but still bright and happy. It stopped Paul in his tracks. He turned towards her to make sure that he wasn't imagining things and that the voice had, indeed, come from the girl. When he had confirmed this, his face broke out in just about the biggest smile Judy had ever seen.

"Good night!" he repeated and left the rec hall, a renewed bounce in his step.

Judy shot daggers at Angela. She wanted nothing more than to cross the rec hall and slug the girl across the nose, drag her nails down that plain, pretty face of hers. It wouldn't do any good. Best to hold it down inside for the time being. Best to bide her time.

Best to wait for the right moment to strike.

6

"Come on girls!" Bill said. "Water's really warm at night. Trust me!"

He stood in front of an assembly of older girls near the waterfront. All of them were pretty, or at least cute, and none of them looked at all interested. Bill shot a glance over his shoulder to the group of other boys regarding him expectantly. They were counting on him to make this work. His glance wandered and he found Mike and Kenny laughing near one of the docks, sharing a joint. Why weren't the fucks over here helping him? *Assholes.* He sighed and

returned his attention to the girls. "What do you say, huh?"

"I don't know, Billy," Betsy said. She was an attractive brunette that had somehow made herself the de facto leader of this little group of gals. Her arms were folded, closed-off. Bill could tell that he wasn't going to get anywhere with her.

"Why don't you get started without us," she said to a titter of laughter from the assembled girls.

Bill felt his blood begin to boil. "The hell with you, then! You don't know how to have fun anyway." It was a pathetic response, but he didn't have anything else. He stormed off towards the group of boys and took his clothes off. They could still have fun without any girls around.

As he stepped out of his shorts, his wandering eye settled on Mike and Kenny once again. Kenny, in particular. He was remembering a night at camp two years previously. He and Kenny out near the water, no clothes on, no girls around—no one else at *all* around. They still had their fun, and he had certainly learned a few things that night.

When all the boys were naked, they started out towards the water. Bill followed them but didn't go out as far as they did, staying in the shallows. It was cold—he had lied to the girls, obviously. Mike and Kenny had started towards the assembled group of girls once Bill had departed. He wanted to see if they would do any better than he had.

"Any of you ladies interested in a moonlight canoe ride?" Kenny said.

The fucks! They weren't trying to get the girls skinny dipping at all. They were trying to *get some*—and one-on-one, too. Selfish pricks.

The girls, to their credit, didn't seem to be any more interested in this proposal than Bill's. Mike looked at them, trying not to laugh and failing. He was stoned off his ass, and it was obvious.

"Come on," Kenny continued, "I won't try anything, I promise." He locked eyes with Betsy. "How about it, Betsy?"

She shook her head. "I don't think so, Kenny."

Bill smirked. *Good*, he thought. *Get in this cold water with us and freeze your dick off. That'll teach you.*

"Leslie's coming down soon," Betsy said. "Why don't you ask her?"

"Son of a bitch," Bill said to himself. Now there was no chance that Kenny would spend

the rest of the evening with the boys. There's no way he was going to share Leslie with them. He liked the skinny little bitch too much.

"Leslie's coming down?" Kenny said.

Betsy nodded. "Definitely."

Bill turned away then. He no longer cared what the rest of Kenny's night might look like. If his friend wanted to have some alone time with some ditzy broad instead of him, then so be it. Bill splashed out into the cold water towards the other boys.

7

"It's pretty nice out here," Leslie said.

Kenny nodded, looked about the lake. She was right, it was nice. They had taken one of the boats out. All the naked boys had departed. Kenny had no idea where Mike was, probably stoned out of his mind somewhere. That stuff never really affected Kenny all that much. It made him feel light-headed and relaxed, but that's all. It had already worn off.

He turned his attention towards Leslie. She was a slim, trim, attractive young woman and she had a playful attitude around boys. He had a shot with her—he could feel it. But she was all the way over there on the other side of the boat. If only there were something that he could do to get her close to him. The idea came to him.

"Ever been out on the lake this late before?" he asked.

She shook her head. "No." Looked out at the water. "The lake kinda creeps me out. A little bit, you know."

"Well, you should be creeped out."

She frowned.

"I'm serious," he said. "That stuff about the Horned Serpent? It's real."

"Come on," Leslie said.

"No, I'm telling the truth. That story that Meg told really happened."

"She's just trying to scare the little kids. Tells it every summer!"

Kenny nodded. "She tells it because it's true. Yeah, sure, she wants to scare the kids—

she's like that—but it's completely real. The native tribes around here knew about it. Knew to stay away from this lake."

He paused and looked out at the large, dark body of water once again. This late, this dark, he could barely see the waterfront. A fine layer of mist had blossomed up out of the depths and settled over the lake. It was eerily quiet.

"Do you think that the Serpent completely changes into a girl?" he said. "Or do you think only part of it changes? I mean, does the head and part of the body turn into the girl while the rest stays a snake? Like a puppet, you know? Does it bob up out of the water like the Loch Ness Monster?" He imitated a water beast with one hand. "Does it snatch you out of your boat?" He snapped at his other hand with the "mouth" of the improvised hand/water beast.

"Stop it," Leslie said.

Kenny smiled and lowered his hands. Clicked his tongue. Shrugged. "Even if it isn't true, this lake is full of snakes. Water snakes, you know? It's a good thing I'm out here with you. You know, to protect you?"

"Dream on, Kenny," she said.

She looked away from him, out towards the water, but he could tell that she was afraid. He had scared her good. It would only take another tiny nudge and she would be his. Slowly, stealthily, he reached down outside the boat and rapped on its side three times. When Leslie turned towards him, he made a good show of looking about, looking concerned. Worried. Scared, even.

"What was that?" she said.

"That's just what I was gonna ask you!" he said. "You heard it, too?"

"Fuck you! What was that?!"

"I don't know, but I got a pretty good idea." He turned scared eyes towards the water. Chattered his teeth in an exaggerated manner. Another idea began to form in his diseased brain. Leslie in the water with him, clutching onto him for safety. Slowly, he began to rock the boat from side to side. "Oh shit, I think we're gonna tip over! We'll be in the water with that thing. The Horned Serpent!"

"Don't you dare, Kenny!" she said.

"Too late!"

With one final push, the boat toppled upside down, dunking them into the water. Leslie

yelped in fear as she went down. Kenny stifled a laugh as his head went underwater. When he

came up, Leslie was already swimming away from him and the boat. He grabbed hold of the overturned boat and shook his head.

"Where you going?!" he called out. "It was just a joke! Come on, Leslie!"

"Fuck you!" she called back to him as she swam towards shore.

Kenny watched her go. Sighed. *Well, that backfired,* he thought. He rapped playfully on the boat and just stayed where he was for a moment. He was alone now. Totally alone.

And yet. It didn't seem like it. Didn't feel like it. It felt like something was watching him. Watching him from the blackness of the water. Watching and waiting.

Waiting for the right time to strike.

Suddenly, Kenny didn't want to be out on the water anymore. He wanted to be back on shore where no Horned Serpent could follow him. Briefly he considered leaving the boat where it was and just swimming back to shore like Leslie had. But if he did that, he might get in trouble for leaving the boat out here on the water. No, he had to take the boat back. He was pretty sure that the oar was under the boat and it would only take a moment to flip it over. He was strong enough to do it.

"Yeah," he said. "Piece of cake."

He took another moment to see if anyone—any*thing*—was

watching him. When he was satisfied that there was nothing but darkness around him, he disappeared under the water and popped up under the overturned boat.

It was pitch black under the canopy of the boat. His mind was filled with everything that had scared him as a child. Every creature that had slithered underneath his bed, every monster that had hidden in his closet. In this moment, it felt like they were all just on the other side of the boat, waiting for him to reemerge.

But that was childish. It was stupid. There was nothing out there but water and night creatures. *Yes,* his mind insisted, *night creatures like the ones in your room after midnight when you were a kid.*

He shook his head, trying to banish such thoughts from his mind. Tried to replace them with fantasies—Leslie underneath the boat with him, Leslie naked and sidling up beside him, Billy in the same position two years ago. But it was no good. Leslie and Billy were replaced with the Horned Serpent rising up from the depths to snatch him in its grip and drag him down.

Knock, knock, knock.

Three knocks on the outside of the boat right near his head. Three knocks. That was all. His mind began to race—*it's the Horned Serpent it's come for me I have to close my eyes I have to pretend I'm not here*—and his teeth began to chatter for real this time.

There was movement in the water. Something moving under the gentle waves from the outside, going under and then rising up in the darkness under the boat with him. Some nightmare from the depths. Some ancient childhood fear. Some *shape.*

He couldn't see what it was, but he knew it was there. It had risen up out of the water to face him. And it was slowly moving towards him.

"Stay back!" he shouted. "Go away!"

He pissed his trunks, the muscles just giving up and letting go, momentarily warming the water. The shape—The Horned

Serpent—was perhaps an inch away from his nose now. He could smell it. It smelled like children, like kids playing in the water, splashing around.

He frowned. This wasn't some monster. It was a *person*.

"Who are you?" he asked.

His answer was a shot to the groin with something strong and heavy. *The oar*. It slammed into his balls and he crumpled in the water. Quick as a snake, the person in the water with him raised the oar and hit him over the head with it.

Kenny was dazed. Suddenly he couldn't hear anything but a high-pitched ring in his ears. He made to grab his head when the oar came down again, this time breaking three of his fingers. He yelped in pain and reared back, trying to get away from his attacker, only succeeding in running into the boat. The oar came down a third time, slamming into the back of his head. There was a crunch as his skull collapsed into his brain.

He made several gurgling sounds as light exploded behind his eyes. A fourth blow turned the back of his head into mush and he thought—and felt—no more.

8

Hal was head lifeguard at Camp Arawak. He'd seen a lot of strange stuff in the water over the years. He'd found condoms in boats, rubber ducks, a baseball bat or two. And garbage, garbage, garbage.

It was a fairly typical summer morning for Hal. He was always cleaning for the little peckerheads after some party the night before. They always snuck out to the waterfront to drink, smoke, do drugs, and fuck. It was always the same.

A fine layer of mist covered the lake this morning. It drifted out from the water towards land. The dock was filthy. The peckerheads must have had one hell of a party last night. There was garbage all over the place. *Pick this up, pick that up.* Always the same. The little bastards.

And they had left a boat out unmoored! It looked like it had drifted to shore sometime before dawn. Something else that he would have to take care of!

Clean this, clean that. Always the same.

Hal wandered towards the boat, hopping off the dock and kicking a baseball out of his way. When he reached the boat, and saw what was inside, he nearly threw up.

Lying in the boat was a dead body. A boy. He was lying on his side, eyes and mouth open. The back of his head had been crushed. It was merely a large, open hole. As Hal watched, a water snake slithered over the body's shoulder into the hole in the back of its head and then emerged from the open, silently screaming mouth. It flicked its tongue about, tasting the air as it did.

That was enough for Hal. He turned, bent over, and lost his breakfast between his legs.

CHAPTER
FIVE
LITTLE BOYS

1

Mel looked worried—not just worried, but on the verge of panic. Subtle panic. Ronnie had known the man long enough to spot it right off.

It was still morning. The medical examiner was busy loading Kenny's body into the meat wagon. A small crowd had gathered around the waterfront, but the counselors were doing a good job of keeping everyone back. Ronnie nodded to Susie and Marie, who were distracting most of the girls—*Where is Meg?* Ronnie thought and shook his head—while Geno was talking to most of the boys.

Mel, Ronnie, and Ben stood near the ambulance when Officer Frank Breton approached them. Ronnie knew Breton. He was a good guy, personable, and never a bully. He was slim but strong, with dark hair and a mustache that seemed glued on, at least to Ronnie's eyes. Mel started talking to the police officer even before the young man had reached them.

"Gotta be an accident, right?" he said.

Ronnie narrowed his eyes but didn't say anything. Breton

had a neutral look on his face, as if he were playing a particularly challenging game of poker.

"I'm no expert," he said. "The medical examiner will have more to say once the autopsy is complete."

"But it had to be an accident," Mel continued. "Boy's out swimming late at night, he gets tired, one of those damn speedboats owned by the rich folks across the water comes along and splat." He took the cigar out of his mouth for emphasis. "Propeller could do that to the boy's head, am I right?"

Breton seemed to consider it. "It's possible, but I wouldn't rule anything out."

"These things have happened before," Mel said.

"Mel, I don't—" Ronnie said.

"Happens all the time," Mel cut him off.

Breton nodded. "It has happened, that's true."

Mel sighed. "How long do you think the autopsy will take?"

"You know how it works around here," Breton said. "They're short-staffed. At least a week. They'll put the kid on ice until they have the time."

"I'm sure they'll decide that it's an accident." Cigar back between his lips again. "It's drunk rich kids out on the water at night in one of those damn speedboats. We got rid of them here at the camp after that accident all those years ago. And this is an accident just like that one. You'll see. Now, if you'll excuse me, I have the unpleasant task of informing the boy's parents." With that, he was off, heading towards his office. And no doubt a good drink or two.

Ronnie watched him go, eyes narrowed. Breton was by his side, doing the same thing. The two men shared a look. Breton didn't have to say anything—Ronnie could read his mind.

"He's just worried about bad publicity," he said. "He'll accept whatever the medical examiner finds as the truth."

Breton nodded. "What were you about to say before he bit your head off there?"

Ronnie sighed and hesitated for a moment. It almost felt like a betrayal to say anything, but he figured he had to. He wasn't going to lie—or withhold information—from a cop. "Nothing, really. It's just that I remember that kid as being a pretty good swimmer, that's all."

Breton nodded, patted Ronnie on the shoulder, and departed. Ronnie watched him go before his gaze settled on Ben, who hadn't said a single word the whole morning. The old man was looking at the assembled crowd of campers.

And he looked scared.

Ronnie frowned. "What is it, Ben?"

Ben jumped as if he hadn't even known Ronnie was there. He shot the younger man a look, and vigorously shook his head. "Nothing. Nothing at all."

Ronnie said nothing, just continued frowning. Ben shot another look at the crowd, then back at Ronnie.

"Just a shame, that's all," he said. "Too young to die. You understand?"

Ronnie nodded, but he was still frowning. Ben shared an awkward moment with him before making his exit. Ronnie watched him for a second before joining the other counselors in shooing away the assembled crowd. Morning activities would be starting sometime soon.

2

"Nine-six," Judy said as she served the volleyball up into the air and lobbed it over the net to the other side. Angela watched the game passively from the sidelines, not interested, but with nothing else to look at. Sleep hadn't come easy the night before and she was tired today.

"Hiya, Angela," came a voice.

Startled, she turned to find Paul approaching, tennis racquet in hand, sweat visible through his shirt. Angela liked it. He looked sporty, athletic. Handsome, even.

"How's it going?" he asked as he sat down on the bench next to her.

"Alright," she answered right away. It was remarkable how easy it was to talk to him. There was no one else at camp—besides Ricky and, recently, Susie—who she even spoke more than two words to, but Paul was special. It was as if there was something welling up inside her whenever she was around him, some kind of warm feeling that was both exciting and a little scary. "How's it going with you?"

"Could be better," Paul said. "Your cousin just whipped my ass at tennis."

She chuckled and Paul smiled. He had a nice smile.

"I was thinking," he said, paused. (*Was he blushing? Yes, she thought he was. It was adorable.*) "Maybe we could go see the movie in the rec hall tonight. What do you think?"

She frowned. "I thought we all had to go anyway."

"Well, yeah," he said, "we do. But I meant, you know, do you want to see it together?"

The Disney film, *Escape to Witch Mountain*, would unspool in 16mm just after sunset in the rec hall. Angela hadn't exactly been looking forward to it, but now? Was Paul asking her out on a date? Was this really happening? She could feel butterflies in her stomach, bouncing around inside her. Excitement and anxiety built up within, ready to explode.

"So, how 'bout it?" Paul asked. "Wanna go?"

"Alright," Angela said.

"Great!" Paul said. He seemed genuinely excited. It didn't seem like a trick or a mean joke, he really did want to spend time with her. Angela couldn't conceal her own joy and excitement, even though somewhere deep down inside, she could hear the Other Angela speak up with a warning. *Careful. He could be like all the others.*

But the voice was distant, barely audible. It was easy to dismiss.

"Hey, how come Angela gets to talk to the boys while we

have to play volleyball?" Judy said from the court. "What is she, special?"

Angela frowned at the other girl. The game had paused, it seemed, and everyone was looking at Angela and Paul on the sidelines. Suddenly, Angela felt exposed—caught. Instinctively, she crossed her arms over her chest. On the court, Meg joined Judy.

"Doesn't seem fair, does it?" she said. She left the court and headed towards the two of them, a stern look on her face. When she reached them, she turned that screwed up, dour face on Paul. "Don't you have somewhere to be?"

"I'm going," Paul said wearily. Then, more warmly. "See you tonight, Angela."

It took every bit of Angela's power to answer him. She wanted nothing more than to simply shut down, look at the ground, remain silent, but she persevered. "Goodbye."

He smiled at her as he got up from the bench and left. It made her feel good, seeing him smile like that, but the Other Angela spoke up inside her again, louder this time. *Why is he leaving? He knows that Meg is always a bitch to you, so why isn't he sticking around and defending you? What kind of a man is he?*

"Listen, Angela," Meg said, shaking her loose from the Other Angela's grasp, "if you're not going to participate, you better just sit there and do nothing. That does not include talking to boys. Understand?"

Angela looked passively up at Meg, feeling so small that she could be squashed like a bug under the counselor's foot.

"You're not a goddamn prima donna," Meg said.

Susie, who was leading the opposing team on the volleyball court, joined the two of them. She, at least, would defend Angela, it seemed. "So she was talking with a boy, so what? Let's just finish the game so we can get ready for lunch."

Meg challenged Susie with a look for a moment before answering. "Yeah, let's." And left Angela to return to the court.

Susie sat down beside Angela and put an arm around her shoulders. "Are you sure you don't want to play?"

Angela nodded. "Yeah, I'm sure."

"Is there anything else you want to do? Go sailing or something?" She smiled. "Archery?"

Angela offered a small smile of her own. "No, that's all right. I don't mind watching."

"Okay," Susie said. A pat with that warm, comforting arm and she was gone, up from the bench and back out onto the court. Angela watched passively, but the Other Angela wasn't passive. She was angry. *Susie's more of a man than Paul! He won't protect you from Meg. You'll have to do something about her yourself.*

On court, it was Meg's turn to serve and she looked at Angela as she held out the ball and called out the score. "Ten-seven." After that the ball was up in the air and in play.

3

Ben's hand shook as he raised the bottle to his lips. It was past dinner, already dark, and he was on his own time now. He had bought the bottle in town earlier today: Jack Daniels. It had been some time since he had been a regular drinker, and he had never touched the stuff while at camp, working, but this summer was different. This summer, he needed it.

There was a small shack in the woods outside of camp. It had once been a storage shed, but no one used it anymore and it had fallen into ruin over the past few years. That's where Ben had made camp for the evening. He had to get away from everyone else.

This morning, at the waterfront, as the medical examiner had carted away the body of that poor boy, Ben had scanned the crowd of onlooking campers and had spotted the one he had seen fleeing the kitchen after Artie's "accident." The presence of the child had shaken him deeply.

Taking a deep swig of the burning alcohol, he sat down on

the decrepit floor of the shack and let the warmth of the drink fill him up inside. Closing his eyes, he tried to rest, but it was futile. Rest wouldn't come.

He had to do something with the knowledge.

He had considered telling Mel about what he had seen but had hesitated. They were just a child. Maybe it really was an accident. But after the death of the boy during the night, he wasn't so sure.

He had also considered quitting—telling Mel that he had had enough and simply high-tailing it out of camp and back to a world that made sense to him. The death of Artie, and his own promotion to head chef, should have invigorated him—he hadn't liked the man and the extra money was good—but now it gave him no pleasure at all. All he wanted was to be done with it.

All of the shack's windows had been broken over time, and graffiti lined the walls. A strong wind blew in through the window above him and a pile of dead leaves kicked up from the ground and headed for the door. Ben watched the leaves dance in the air. The latch on the door to the shack had been broken ages ago and the door banged open and shut in the wind, making a surprisingly loud noise in the otherwise serene quiet.

Ben focused on the banging door, watching it open and close in the wind, and took another swig of the good burn. Choked and coughed. He was just too old for this kind of thing. He wasn't the right person to hold a secret like this.

But you kept Artie's secret, his conscience told him. *You kept that particular secret for years, didn't you?*

Ben nodded. Yes, he had. But this was, potentially, murder. That was worse, wasn't it? *Was it?* his conscience asked. *Didn't Artie deserve it?*

Ben sighed. He didn't know. How could he know? He wasn't like that. He wasn't like Artie.

The door to the shack banged open and closed and he

caught glimpses of the woods each time it was open. It was like the shutter of a camera—a slow one, to be sure, but a shutter nonetheless—showing him snapshots of the deep woods that surrounded Camp Arawak. It was beautiful out there, but also dangerous. There was something untamed about it. Something primal.

The door shuttered open and Ben saw a figure standing outside the shack in the woods. It was only a silhouette, but he recognized who it was all the same. The bottle dropped from his hand, hit the ground, and rolled towards the door. The wind died down and the door slowly opened and stayed that way, giving him an unobstructed view of the figure.

Suddenly, his mouth was dry. He had no saliva and, once again, he choked and coughed. Struggled to speak.

"I won't tell," he managed. "Whatever happened to Artie, no one will know about it.

Hear me? Nobody will ever know!"

The figure was silent. Still. Ben shifted in place. His back was against the wall, his ass still on the dirty floor, and he couldn't seem to get up.

"As for the boy…" he said. "Well, that was just an accident, wasn't it?" No answer. "Wasn't it?"

When there was still no answer forthcoming, he couldn't keep the look of horror from his face. He was never a good poker player, and he could tell that the child could see all his cards in that particular moment. There was an agonizing few seconds when neither of them moved, remaining on opposite sides of the metaphorical card table. When Ben finally moved, so did the figure.

Ben tried to get up as quickly as he could, using both of his hands to launch himself off the floor. The figure reached down and grabbed Ben's discarded bottle of whiskey. Ben launched himself towards the figure, but the child was ready and swung the bottle at the old man. It smashed across his left temple, drawing blood and throwing the man backwards. He cried out in pain and alarm. Tried to get up again. "Help!"

He was on all fours, feeling desperate, terrified. The figure brought the broken bottle, now an edged weapon, down on Ben's right hand, stabbing right through it. Ben cried out once again, called for help once again. On some level, he knew it was futile. He was too far from camp for anyone to hear him and the chances of someone wandering in the woods nearby at this particular moment was remote at best.

The figure pulled the bottle out of Ben's hand, an eruption of blood following the weapon. Ben looked the figure straight in the eye, teeth clenched for a second before speaking. "You killed that b—"

Before he could finish the sentence, the figure slashed the bottle across his face, shredding his lips and cheeks into ribbons. A water-fall of blood cascaded from Ben's mouth and gums. His tongue had been cut into several pieces as well. The pain was incredible.

As Ben reared back, the figure took another step closer and buried the broken bottle into the old man's stomach. There was a horrid squelching sound as Ben's guts were ripped open. The rank smell that followed as intestinal gases filled his nostrils was almost worse than the pain.

Ben looked the child in the eye once again as he choked on his own blood. Death followed soon after.

4

After the movie, Paul walked Angela back to her bunk. They both enjoyed the film. Angela had never seen it before, but Paul had. He spent most of the time looking at Angela while the film unspooled at the back of the rec hall. While he did want to score this summer, tonight Paul really just wanted to make sure that Angela was having a good time. Based on the big, genuine smile on her face, it looked like she was.

Just as they reached Angela's cabin, Paul took a chance, swinging for the fences, and pulled her aside, into the shadow formed by a large tree off to one side of the bunk. Angela looked confused and a little afraid.

"What are we doing?" she asked.

"I wanna show you something," he said.

Before she had time to react—or run—Paul planted a kiss on her lips. It was a small kiss, little more than a peck, but it felt monumental. Angela had barely been speaking to anyone a week ago and now Paul had been able to plant one on her. *Score*.

She looked even more confused as she looked away from him, off into the darkness of the camp. Paul frowned.

"You're not mad, are you?" he asked.

She shook her head. "No." A pause, like she was a computer processing data. "I gotta go now."

"Can I have another one?" he asked. When she looked at him, that confused look still on her face, he cocked his head to one side. "You know, another kiss?"

She didn't speak, but she nodded. And he kissed her again. This one was a little longer, a little more intimate, but still chaste. When it was over, Angela still looked confused. Her eyes were fixed on anything except him.

"Good night," she said as she left his side.

"Night," he called after her.

A second later she was gone, disappearing into her cabin. Paul smiled to himself and made to leave. Judy cornered him before he had a chance.

"Hey, Paul," she said with a mischievous smile on her face.

"Hi, Judy," he said and managed to not sigh in frustration.

"You and Angela sure are becoming quite an item."

He frowned. "So what?"

Judy shrugged. "I just didn't think that she was your type." Sidled up closer to him. "Know what I mean?"

Paul couldn't help but look at her chest. She had developed since the previous summer, that was for sure. He was tempted, no denying that, but he resisted. "Good night, Judy." Untangling himself from her non-contact contact, he left, feeling more than a little good about himself.

5

"Judy," Ricky called from the shadows.

Paul had just left her side and Judy was about to head into her cabin. She sighed and turned to regard Ricky as he took a step out of the darkness. Crossed her arms. "What do you want, Ricky?"

He had a confident smile on his face as he approached her. It looked like he had just taken a shower—he was clean and neat. But it was that confidence that made him appear different to Judy.

"We had some good times last summer, didn't we?" he asked.

She shrugged. "I guess."

"Oh, come on. You know we did."

They had, in fact. Judy remembered having a great time with Ricky the previous summer, but she had moved on since then. "That was then, this is now."

"What's that supposed to mean?" Ricky said.

"It means that I'm looking for men and you're still a little boy. Get it?"

He scoffed. "Little boy?" Shook his head, turned away. When he turned back to her, he gestured off towards the boys' cabins. "What about Paul, huh? Is he a man?"

She shrugged again. "Maybe."

"That's bullshit. You just like him because he likes my cousin."

She didn't answer him. How could she have thought that Ricky had been full of confidence a moment ago? He was a *boy* and nothing more. A child.

"Admit it!" Ricky said. There was a flash of real anger in his eyes and Judy took a step back. "You're just picking on Angela! You don't care about Paul!"

"I don't have to tell you shit," she said. "Good night." With that, she turned away from him and headed up the small set of stairs to her cabin. She heard him take one single step behind her, but didn't turn to look back. Sure enough, he didn't follow her. He stayed on that one step watching her leave like the little boy that he was.

A real man would have stopped her.

6

That evening, when all the boys were back in their bunk, Paul sat on his bed singing to himself. The other boys were gathered around another one of the beds, doing God knows what. Paul thought that he was singing quietly—some love song or another; might have been something by The Beatles—but Ricky, who was in the center of the group of gathered boys, turned and shushed him. It was a fierce, decisive shush and Paul shut up. Frowned and got up from his bed to see what was going on.

He found the other boys gathered around Mozart's bed. The nerdy kid was passed out, mouth gaping open, a line of drool trailing down one cheek like an open wound. One of the other boys, Baron, stifled a laugh with one hand. Paul noticed that the boy held a sock in his other hand. Paul looked at Ricky, who was holding a can of shaving cream.

"What's going on?" he whispered.

Ricky gave him a dismissive wave before spraying a good amount of shaving foam into the open palm of Mozart's hand. He turned to Baron, nodded, and whispered, "OK, go for it. But don't wake him up."

Baron nodded back and raised the dirty sock over Mozart's nose. He just let the bottom edge of the sock tickle the sleeping boy's nostrils. Back and forth. Paul could practically feel the split threads of the sock on his own nose and instinctively ran a hand across it.

On the bed, Mozart made the same motion, bringing his outstretched, open hand to his face to find out what was tickling him in his sleep. Baron pulled the sock away at the last possible moment and Mozart hit himself in the face with a handful of shaving cream.

As everyone, Paul included, started to laugh, Mozart sat bolt upright in bed, dazed and confused. He looked about at all the laughing boys, at his hand, then rubbed at his face, finally discovering what was going on.

"What's the matter, Motz?" Ricky said. "Five-o-clock shadow?"

"You bastards!" Mozart said.

He got up from the bed as the others got out of his way. Ricky couldn't stop laughing and jumped up on the nearest bed, hopping up and down.

"I'll fucking kill you!" Mozart said.

He went to grab something from the cubicle over his bed. At first, Paul couldn't see what it was. Mozart grabbed it from under a stack of shorts and folded shirts and turned to face Ricky. Paul could see what it was now: a hunting knife, sheathed in brown leather. Mozart pulled the knife out like a professional, brandishing the weapon at Ricky.

Ricky didn't seem phased at all. He pulled a mock fear face and pretended to bite his nails in terror. Mozart looked like he was about to strike with the weapon when a voice called from the main door of the cabin.

"Hey!" Gene said.

Everyone turned to look at the counselor as he closed the door behind him and entered the cabin. "What, are you kidding me?" He crossed the room and grabbed the knife and sheath from Mozart's hands. "Are you nuts or something?"

He went to his own bed, and the cubicle above it, tucked the knife and sheath under his own clothes. Shaking his head as he turned to Mozart, he sighed. "You'll see that at the end of the summer, if you're lucky. Idiot."

Ricky hopped off the bed to land next to Mozart. Chuckled. Clapped a derisive hand on Mozart's shoulders and laughed.

"That the kind of crack counseling they teach you at Packanack Lodge?" he said.

There was much laughter, Paul's included. They had all learned that Gene had some counselor training earlier in the summer in New Jersey. *Who had to train to be a camp counselor?* Paul thought, still laughing.

"Cute. Cute. Maybe I should ask Ronnie what he thinks I should do about all you," Gene said, still shaking his head. "Right, now everybody into bed."

Reluctantly, they all climbed into their beds. Mozart used a towel to wipe the shaving cream off his face. He didn't look happy.

Paul could sympathize, but he had to admit that it was funny. With this, and riding the high of stealing a kiss from Angela, he went to bed with a smile on his face. Sleep came quickly and easily. The dreams that followed were good ones.

7

Long after everyone else was asleep, Mozart snuck out of the bunk and wandered around the camp. This late, with the grounds deserted, a stillness and quiet settled on everything like morning dew. Mozart snatched a rock off the ground and threw it as far as he could, which didn't amount to much.

He sighed and kicked another small mound of rocks out of his way as he stomped through the camp. Why did everyone always pick on him? Was it his face? His glasses? His physical shortcomings? What was it?

He knew that he was a nerd. He preferred video games, *Star Trek*, and reading to playing baseball or archery, or anything else outdoorsy. That was probably why the other boys picked on him, especially the older ones. Because he was different.

Just once he would like to be the one picking on someone. Just once he would like to feel the exhilaration of that, the feeling of superiority.

The sound of movement shook him out of his own thoughts. He looked around, eyes wide. Was it some kind of animal? Some kind of predator? He heard it again and could tell that it was several things moving in the darkness around him.

His mind immediately went to wolves—a pack of wolves on the prowl—out for boy meat. This, he knew, was stupid. There hadn't been wolves around here for decades, but out here, in the dark, it didn't seem so implausible. A pack of wolves, big and grey. Dangerous. They were circling him, sticking to the shadows so as not to be seen.

Mozart could feel his heart racing, could feel every hair on his body stand straight up in terror. Whatever it was, it was close, and moving. He took a pathetic stance and got ready to fight, raising his fists and breathing heavily.

When he saw the culprits, he felt stupid and lowered his fists, uttering a sigh of relief. Slinking out of the dark was a group of three boys, all of them younger than him. When they saw him, a panicked look crossed their faces and they began to bolt.

"Wait," Mozart said, "I'm not gonna tell on you or anything."

The boys stopped and eyed him with suspicion. "Promise?" one of them asked. Mozart was pretty sure the boy's name was Clark. He nodded and assured them that he wasn't going to rat them out to the counselors.

"What are you guys doing out here anyway?" he asked.

Clark shrugged and showed Mozart a handful of firecrackers. "We were gonna go find some frogs by the pond and see if we can blow 'em up."

Mozart chuckled.

Clark shared a look with the other two boys—*Bobby and George? Was that their names?*—as if conferring with them silently. He nodded, then looked back at Mozart. "Wanna come?"

Mozart thought about it for a second before shrugging. "What the hell?" The boys looked delighted and Mozart followed them when they made their way to the pond.

CHAPTER
SIX
CONSEQUENCES

1

By the waterfront, there were benches to sit on arranged like stadium seating. They faced the water, allowing some rest for campers who needed it while still letting them see everyone playing in the water.

It was a bright, new day and Angela was sitting on the lowest bench, passively watching the girls splashing in the water. There were considerably less of them out there. A lot of parents had come and picked up their children after Kenny's death, but the ones remaining seemed to still be having a good time. As Angela was idly thinking about all of this, a pair of hands wrapped around her head from behind and covered her eyes.

"Guess who?" a voice asked in her left ear.

She knew immediately who it belonged to but wanted to mess around with him for a second or two. "Um, Ricky."

"Nope!"

"Um… Burt Reynolds!"

"Getting closer."

"I give up."

The hands disappeared from her eyes and Paul sat down on the bench next to her, a big smile on his face. "Surprise!"

"Who are you?" Angela said, managing to keep a straight face. Paul mocked disappointment. They both smiled and shared a moment of comfortable silence together. She liked this. Liked spending time with Paul. He was a little strange sometimes, and she wasn't sure that she liked it when he forced that kiss on her, but he was handsome and fun to be around.

This pleasant feeling was short-lived when Judy approached the two of them. She looked beautiful as usual in a one-piece bathing suit, her still-dry hair indicating that she had probably just been lounging in the sun rather than swimming.

"Well, well," she said, "if it isn't the two lovebirds." Her mean eyes went from Paul's face down to his crotch, then over to Angela. "Hey, Angela, he stick it to you yet?" Chuckled to herself. "On a scale of 1 to 10, how small was it?"

"Why don't you get out of here," Paul snapped.

Judy scoffed, but left the two of them and headed towards the dock. Paul shook his head. "She can be a real jerk sometimes." Despite his words, Angela could see that he was looking at her ass as she walked away. She tried to hide the disappointment from her face—in case he ever stopped ogling Judy's body—and looked towards the water. Judy was now by Meg's side, talking to the counselor. It looked like a conspiracy to Angela. She narrowed her eyes.

At the dock, Meg listened carefully to Judy before looking towards Angela and Paul. She crossed her arms for a moment, then started towards them.

"Uh oh," Paul said, "looks like the Wicked Witch of the West is headed this way. I better get outta here."

He got up from the bench and left. Inside, Angela was shocked. *He's leaving! Why is leaving me alone again? He knows how mean Meg is. He knows that she doesn't like me! Why is he doing this to me?* On the outside, her face remained impassive, blank. A defense mechanism.

"Not going into the water again, huh, Angela?" Meg said once she reached Angela. "What's the matter, don't you like to swim? *Can* you swim?"

Of course she could swim. Meg must have thought she was stupid. But she couldn't swim with all these people around. Not with what was between her legs. She did a good job of hiding it, but if she were all wet, it would probably be easy to spot. There was no way she was getting into the water when everyone else was around.

"Angela," Meg said, "I'm talking to you. Are you going in the water or aren't you? Huh?!"

Anger was building up in Angela. Deep down, in that black place inside, the voice of the Other Angela spoke up. *Do something! She's worse than Judy. Judy might be a bitch, but she's just a child. Meg is an adult and should know better. So do something! Slap her. Hit her!*

"I am waiting for an answer!" Meg said. "Yes or no?"

When Angela refused to do anything but look passively up at the counselor towering over her, Meg grit her teeth and actually stomped a foot into the sand. "Goddamnit, Angela, answer me! What is wrong with you?! Answer me!"

"Jesus Christ, what the hell is going on here?"

It was Ronnie, approaching the two of them with a look of concern on his face. *A real adult,* Angela thought to herself as the voice of the Other Angela slowly dissipated. *Thank God.*

"The little bitch won't answer me," Meg said, gesturing towards Angela.

Ronnie looked at her for a second, a deep frown on his face, then turned to regard Angela. "You alright, Angela?"

She gave a curt nod but didn't say anything. Ronnie nodded back and looked at Meg. He raised his eyebrows.

"I want to see you in my shack right after swim period," he told her. "Now get back to your post."

Meg laughed derisively, amazed. Shook her head. But she left and Angela found herself relieved. Ronnie put a hand on her shoulder. When she first came to camp, she probably would have flinched if he had touched her, but not anymore. It was a comforting gesture. His smile was also comforting. He gave her a pat and left.

2

After having a good talk with Meg, Ronnie headed into Mel's office. He had intended to talk with the camp owner about the incident by the waterfront, but found his boss on the phone, so he stood off to one side of the desk and remained quiet.

Mel acknowledged his presence with a nod and said into the phone, "No." A pause. "Thanks for nothing." He hung up with a sigh and grabbed another cigar from the box on his desk, lit it up and stuck it in his mouth. There was a glass filled half full with dark liquid nearby.

Ronnie wasn't even thinking about the altercation between Meg and Angela anymore. He had figured out what the phone call must have been about. "No word?"

Mel shook his head. "Nothing. Not a goddamn thing." Chewed thoughtfully on his cigar.

Ronnie sighed and took a chair opposite the desk. He felt helpless, but tried to think of something that he could do.

"My cousin's not a bad cook," he said after a moment. "I could call her. She could probably get here tomorrow." He shrugged. "She'd have to drag my nephew along, I suppose."

Mel waved a dismissive hand, still not looking at Ronnie. "We still have the seasonal help. They're alright."

Ronnie cocked his head to one side. "You think so? Starting to wonder when we'll see kids dropping dead from food poisoning before the summer's out."

Mel chuckled humorlessly. "That's if there's any left by the end of the summer. How many did we lose this morning?"

"Four," Ronnie answered right away. He had seen the kids off himself, handing them over to their parents at practically first light.

"Jesus, one kid dead alongside a chef, another chef missing."

"Ben's sister doesn't know where he is?"

Mel shook his head. "Hasn't seen him since he left for here." He tapped the desk in front of him with the end of the cigar, leaving ash in its wake.

"Do you think he could be blabbing to somebody about the accidents?" Ronnie asked.

"No, I don't think so. Ben's been with me longer than anybody. He's not the type to talk. Keep his mouth shut even if he had a mouthful of bees."

"So what do you think happened?"

Mel seemed to give it some real thought before answering. "I think somebody did something to him."

"Did something? Like what?"

"Some kind of 'accident,' maybe."

Ronnie scoffed. "Are you telling me that you don't think that these deaths are accidents?"

"No, no," Mel said, getting up from his desk. "I don't want that kind of talk getting around, you hear me? These are nothing but accidents. There's no way we could have prevented any of them. Understand?"

Ronnie nodded.

"All I'm saying," Mel continued, "is that Ben might have also had himself a little accident. Bad luck. That's all it is."

"Right," Ronnie said. "I understand."

He got up to leave. Mel reached out across the desk and grabbed him by the shoulder.

"Was there something you wanted from me?" Mel asked.

Ronnie shook his head. "It wasn't important."

Mel met his gaze and neither of them said anything for a moment. Finally, Mel let go of him and gestured towards the exit. "Don't forget to close the door on your way out. I don't want some kind of accident to blow in here on the fucking wind."

3

Later in the day, Susie was overseeing the girls in her bunk. Both her's and Meg's bunks had been consolidated into one since they had lost a number of campers over the last few days. Most of the girls were waiting in line to take showers after swim period, but Angela sat quietly on her bed, just watching the other girls.

Judy had just finished showering and she wandered into the main room of the cabin wearing a robe and toweling her hair. She noticed Angela watching and flashed a cruel smile, turned to everyone else.

"Hey girls," she said. "Let's not forget to thank Angela for getting Meg into trouble."

"I didn't do anything," Angela said right away. Susie had been considering intervening but decided against it for the moment. Angela had progressed quite a lot over the last week or so. She could handle herself.

"You never do shit," Judy said and retreated to her bed. She grabbed her curling iron from the cubicle above her bed, but before she turned it on, she faced Angela. "Hey, Angela. How come you never take showers when the rest of us do, huh? You queer or something?" Scattered laughter rippled through the cabin.

"Oh, I know what it is," Judy continued. "You haven't reached puberty yet. Is that it? I bet you don't even have your period."

That was enough for Susie. She stood up, hands on hips, and

said, "That's enough, Judy! Angela's allowed to shower in the morning or whenever else she wants to."

But this wasn't enough to stop Judy. She pressed on, taking a step towards Angela as Susie advanced towards her. "Yeah, she takes showers when no one can see she has no hair down below!"

"Judy!" Susie said.

"She's a real carpenter's dream: flat as a board and needs a screw!"

"That's enough!"

Judy finally turned to regard Susie. "Fuck off!"

Susie acted before her mind even had time to process what she was doing. She slapped Judy across the face. Hard. Judy reacted instantly, dropping the curling iron, putting a hand to her cheek, turning and running to her bed, collapsing onto it and burying her head in her pillow. Susie covered her mouth in shock. *Did I mean to do that? I don't think so, but maybe I did. What kind of a person am I?* Before she had time to really think about any of these questions, Angela got up from her bed and approached her.

"I'm going down to see my cousin," she said. "I'll be back for dinner."

Susie could only nod. She had no idea what she would say if she opened her mouth, or even whether she would be able to articulate coherent sounds. Angela nodded back and left the cabin. Susie watched her go, questions circling her brain.

4

Angela had almost reached Ricky's bunk when disaster struck.

Mel coached a few of the boys nearby, giving them some baseball tips. More boys lounged around outside of their cabins, shooting the shit. Mike and Billy were on the roof of their bunk. It was all so very *public* the moment the humiliation came.

Angela didn't acknowledge anyone else as she approached her cousin's bunk. Her mind was elsewhere, contemplating the scene that had unfolded in her own bunk only moments ago. Why did everyone have it out for her? Did they suspect the truth? Did they already know? It was a terrifying prospect and inside Angela was trembling.

Outside, her face and body gave none of this away. She was as still and robotic as she always was, totally composed. When the water balloon hit her in the face, she was completely unprepared.

The balloon exploded square in the forehead, drenching her face, her hair and her shirt. It had been thrown fast, hard, and she fell over backwards, landing on her ass with a jolt. There was another kind of explosion just after the first: laughter. It came from several of the boys gathered nearby and from the roof of one of the cabins.

It was about this time that Angela realized that the balloon had not been filled with water. It was warm, hot and sticky. Her eyes began to burn.

"You like that, Angela?!" Billy called out from the roof, hands cupped around his mouth so that everyone could hear him. "That ain't water! It's piss!" More laughter.

"Yeah," Mike added, "all the guys in our bunk contributed!"

The two of them nearly doubled over with laughter. More of it came from the boys lounging out in front of their cabins and the boys that Mel was coaching.

"Look at Angela!" Mozart said, pointing at her. A group of three younger boys near him laughed loud and long. "Classic!"

"Angela!"

It was Ricky. He ran from his bunk to his cousin but barely paused by her side before taking a few steps towards the older boy's bunk.

"You fucking bastards are gonna pay for this!" he called out, an accusing finger pointed in their direction. "Cocksuckers! Pricks! I'm gonna fight you, chickenshits!"

Angela's eyes hurt. She wiped the sticky urine out of them as best she could, but it wasn't enough. Suddenly, she couldn't see anything anymore, but she could hear someone approaching. Instinctively, she cowered in fear. The Other Angela inside her cried out, *Coward! Get up! Don't let them see you like this! Fight back!*

She pushed the voice down, drowned it out. When the person approaching reached her, he handed her a handkerchief. She could tell that it was Paul and was grateful. Wiping the piss out of her eyes, she could see once again. Could see Ricky going nuts, screaming at Bill and Mike. Could see Mel approaching her cousin and grabbing him by the shoulders.

"I'll kick your goddamn assess all over this camp, you fucks!" Ricky said.

"Take it easy, kid," Mel said. He was clearly having trouble restraining the boy. Ricky was stronger than he looked.

"Those pricks!" Ricky said. "I'll kill 'em!"

"You boys come down from there!" Mel said.

A bee buzzed around Bill's head and he swatted at it, looking scared. Mike chuckled, a big, dumb smile on his face.

"Shut up, man," Billy said. "You know I'm allergic."

"Get down here!" Mel reiterated.

Bill and Mike sighed and climbed down from the roof. When they were on the ground and approaching, Ricky spoke up again. "Those motherfuckers keep picking on my cousin."

"That's bullshit," Bill said.

"That's enough," Mel said. "Now, I saw the whole thing. That was a mean trick you two pulled. She could have gotten hurt. Could have fallen over and broken her goddamn neck."

Billy tried to maintain a straight face while Mike rolled his eyes. Ricky made a move to attack, but Mel held him back.

"Ronnie's gonna hear about this," Mel said, "and there's going to be no canteen for a whole week." He regarded Ricky. "And that goes for you, too, on account of that filthy mouth of yours."

"What?!" Ricky said.

"If I ever hear anything happening like this again," Mel continued, ignoring Ricky, "I'm gonna throw the whole bunch of you out of here, and don't think that I don't mean it. You understand?"

After some reluctance, he got nods from all three of them. With a nod back, he continued. "Now go get ready for dinner."

Billy and Mike retreated to their bunk as Mel and Ricky headed over to Angela and Paul. Mel knelt down to speak to Angela.

"Are you alright?" he asked.

Angela didn't answer. She just realized that now she had to take a shower before dinner. It filled her with terror. She prayed that the rest of the girls were done and that none of them were lingering in the area while she cleaned herself up.

"She'll be okay," Paul said when he realized that Angela wasn't going to answer.

Ricky sat down beside the two of them as Mel stood up, straining to do so. He gave them a curt nod. "Alright. Get cleaned up." Checked his watch. "Almost time for dinner," he said again. There was nothing else he could think of, it seemed.

He left them alone. After another moment, Angela found the courage to stand up. To go back to her bunk. To take a quick shower. Mercifully, most of the other girls had already left for dinner.

5

The next day, after a morning run, Billy returned to his bunk. He was dripping sweat and a little tired, but he was also feeling pumped. He had been down since Kenny's death, but that piss balloon to Angela's face yesterday had been quite the pick-up. Despite getting in trouble, it had raised his spirits considerably.

Mike and some of the other guys were getting their gear

together as Billy entered the cabin. He smiled at his friend. "What are you guys up to today?"

"We gotta a game against the counselors," Mike said, grabbing his bat. "Wanna join us?"

"Maybe," Bill said, an idea formulating in his head as everyone else left the bunk. He rubbed his stomach. "Gotta take a wicked dump, though. I don't think breakfast did me any favors this morning."

Mike chuckled. "I know what you mean. Alright, pal, if you feel up to it, join us on the field. We'll bring you in as a ringer."

He saluted him and Billy saluted back. After that, Mike was gone along with all the other guys. Bill was alone, just the way he wanted it. He did not, in fact, need to take a wicked dump. He went to his cubicle and fished around under a folded stack of shirts and found what he was looking for, an issue of *Hustler* from last year. Beaming down at it for a moment, he kissed the cover and headed into the bathroom.

After making sure that no one was in there, either, he chose his favorite stall—the middle one—and went inside, dropping his shorts and underwear and sitting down on the toilet. His dick was already hard when he sat down, and he turned to the center pictorial. Billy liked the ones with one girl and multiple guys the most, gang-bangs and group scenes, and this pictorial was one of the best he'd come across.

Holding the magazine open one-handedly like an expert, he gave extra special attention to his prick and balls. He was already moaning. This was going to be a quick one, he could tell. It had been several days since he'd had enough alone time to do it, and being all worked up this morning had done the trick.

About a minute later, he was convinced that someone else was with him in the bathroom. He thought he could hear the faint noise of someone tip-toeing around. Holding onto his dick like it was a precious jewel, he stopped what he was doing and listened intently. When he heard nothing, he returned to his business.

Another minute later and he was ready to erupt. It would only be a few seconds now. He was on the very precipice of ecstasy when he heard something behind and above him. It was a ripping sound, as if someone was cutting the mesh window open with a knife.

"Hey," he shouted, "who is that?!"

There was no response, at least not from a human being, but he could hear a loud buzzing. Frowning, he folded the magazine, one-handedly once again. He didn't see the bees until one landed on his inflated balls. Uttering a sharp, girlish scream, he dropped the magazine and swatted at the bee. He only succeeded in scaring the insect, and it stung him in the left testicle.

The pain was intense. It was so bad that he didn't react at all when an entire beehive dropped into the toilet right between his legs. There was a watery splash, and an army of angry bees swarmed into his face.

Terror raced through his veins. It was followed quickly by pain as the first bee stung him. Then another. And another. Dozens of them in rapid succession—his face, his neck, the engorged shaft of his penis, his inner thighs.

His arms flailed about in pain, terror, and panic. His nostrils were filled with the smell of pollen. He couldn't breathe, his throat was closing. Coughing, he went for the stall door, almost tripping over his shorts and underwear wrapped around his ankles. The door had been jammed from the outside.

There *had* been someone in the bathroom with him! The fucker had jammed the door!

His brain was little more than animal instinct at this point as the number of stings on his body reached the hundreds. He could no longer breathe and, after a few attempts to knock the door off its hinges, he dropped to his hands and knees to try to crawl out under the stall door. As he pushed himself through the gap, he could feel the insects in his hair, on his back, in the crack of his ass. They were everywhere. And they were all stingers and fury.

He could taste freedom—his head and arms were out of the stall. Catching a glimpse of himself in the mirror of the bathroom gave him a shock. *What's that thing crawling out from under the bathroom stall? Some kind of monster!*

That was *him*. That bloated, crawling nightmare. How could that be him? But it was true. That thing was him, and he was dying. He could feel his lungs inflating, trying to get air. Every vein in his body ached for relief. They felt like they were going to explode.

Billy made it halfway out of the stall—his exposed, red ass and legs still inside—when he collapsed to the tile floor. He convulsed, let out a pathetic cry, and expired.

6

Ricky watched with horror as his cousin dropped a beehive into the restroom of the older boy's cabin. He was hidden in a grouping of trees some distance away, but he could tell that it was Angela all right. She looked crazed, her eyes wide and scary. Like an animal.

Had she killed Kenny? It didn't seem possible, but he couldn't deny the evidence of his own eyes. Billy's screams echoed from the bunk. Angela stood where she was for a moment, looking off into nothingness much like her aunt, before she seemed to shake herself out of it. After taking a look around and seeing no one—Ricky was well hidden—she ran off.

Ricky stayed where he was for a moment before making his own escape. He didn't want anyone to think he had done it.

Returning to his bunk, he couldn't keep the troubled look off his face. Could it be possible? Could his cousin have just killed Billy? Because there was no way that Bill could have survived an attack from that many bees. Everybody knew that he was allergic.

When Paul asked him what was wrong, Ricky waved it away like it was nothing.

Inside, he was full of questions. One thing was certain, though.

Now it was even more important to keep Angela safe.

CHAPTER
SEVEN

LEGACY OF MADNESS

1

Ricky made sure that he chose the telephone furthest away from any of the cabins when he made the call. It was a pay phone near the rec hall, sitting outside near a grouping of trees. Most of the other kids either gawked at the removal of yet another dead body from the camp, or were off doing some kind of activity. He saw no one nearby.

It took him three tries to reach his mother, Martha Thomas. When he finally got a hold of her, she seemed to be having one of her more spacey days. Ricky sighed.

"Hi, mom," he said.

"Richard!" his mother said. "How is camp, my darling? Still taking care of my little angel, I hope, hmm?"

"Mom, I need you to listen to me."

"Why, of course! When have I not listened to you, Richard dear?"

Ricky restrained himself from mentioning several times that he remembered right off the top of his head. "Do you remember what you told me about Grandpa Peter?"

A pause before she answered. "Yes. Why, yes, I believe that I do. Interesting man my father was."

"Interesting, yeah," Ricky said. "He was… He was hospitalized, right?"

"That is true, yes."

"You said that he was acting funny before they put him away."

"Well, he was a funny man," Martha said, "always cracking jokes that would make us girls laugh our heads off!"

He sighed once again. "That's not what I mean. He was… acting strange, right?"

Another pause from his mother. "He was. He had… moments."

"Did he ever hurt anyone?" Ricky asked.

"Well, the state accused him of many things, but they couldn't prove anything because it just wasn't true." A spacey pause. "Yes, that's just what they said."

"Some kids in grade school told me that he killed people," Ricky said. "A few people. Is that true?"

"There were a few deaths," she said, "that's true. But they were accidents, nothing more."

Ricky closed his eyes and stamped a fist against the post that the pay phone was nailed to. Bit his lower lip. "Suppose it was true, though. Just suppose." How could he approach this? "That sort of thing, you don't think it runs in the family, do you?"

"Why, no, my dear! Talk like that is just silly!" Quieter now. "Yes, that's just what it is, silly."

He could tell that she had slipped into one of her strange fits. "Mom? Come on, mom."

"How is camp, Richard?" she repeated herself, all bright and cheery.

He opened his eyes, a single tear running down his face. That one moment, that slip, had convinced him that it was all true. Madness did run in his family. *Should I tell her about what's going on here? Would it do any good?*

Probably not, but it wouldn't hurt to give it a try. He sighed one final time and spoke up. "Mom, there's something going on here. I don't know if we should be here anymore."

2

"Finished," Mel said.

He and Ronnie were in the art building, surrounded by sculptures, drawings, and other pieces of art mostly made by children. The door to the building was open and Mel stood on the threshold, looking out into the chilly late evening air. They had lost dozens of kids today after the discovery of Billy's body.

"That's all there is to it," he continued. "Finished. Wiped out." He turned to Ronnie, rubbing his hands together. There was no cigar, either in his mouth or his hand, a rarity for him. "How many are left?"

Ronnie consulted his clipboard for a moment. "Looks like about twenty-five."

Mel shook his head in despair. "Might as well pack everything up and shut down. Nobody's ever gonna send their kids here again."

"Why don't we finish the summer, Mel?" Ronnie said, offering the smallest of smiles. That Ronnie, always trying to find a silver lining. "Tomorrow I'll consolidate the bunks. There's no sense in keeping everyone spread out."

"Yeah," Mel said, not even looking at Ronnie. "Why make things easier for the killer?"

"Hey, don't talk like that. We don't know anything for sure."

"I know!" Mel shouted, turning to him. "I've known all along. I've seen the hate in his eyes." He wandered away again, towards the open door. "But I never did anything about it. Now, though," he shook his head, "I'll stop him for what he's done to me." He slammed a fist into the frame of the door. "I'll stop him!"

"Snap out of it, will ya?" Ronnie said, stepping towards him and putting a hand on his shoulder. "You're talking crazy."

"Yeah," Mel said, "maybe I am. Maybe I'm just… imagining it." But he wasn't. He knew who the killer was. And he knew that they *were* killings, not just accidents like he had been trying to convince everyone else since the beginning.

But he was going to put a stop to it. This was his camp. It was his responsibility. No one else's.

He was going to stop this madness even if it killed him.

3

Angela hadn't been able to stop the Other Angela from taking over. When it happened, it just happened. She had no say in the matter. The anger, the rage, was so powerful, so overwhelming, that she simply surrendered to it and became small as the Other Angela grew to monstrous proportions.

When the Other Angela took over, she was like a snake, slinking into the water to go after Kenny, snatching Mozart's hunting knife from Gene's cubicle while the boys were sleeping, deftly retrieving the beehive with a long stick to take care of Bill. Angela would be impressed if she wasn't so scared.

And yet.

There was a seductive kind of power in letting go, in allowing the Other Angela to take over. Her doppelgänger was certainly more confident than she was, more ready to dole out swift, brutal justice to bullies.

It was late. She had agreed to meet Paul near the boys' cabins, but he hadn't shown up yet, and Angela found herself wandering around the woods near his bunk. *Where is he?*

She heard movement and looked about. Near a grouping of trees beside one of the cabins, she saw Susie. Ducking down into the shadows of the woods, Angela watched and waited, hoping that she wasn't going to be caught.

Susie looked weary. Tired. She pulled a pack of cigarettes

out of her back pocket and lit one up. Took a long drag on it, closed her eyes.

Approaching her from behind was Marie, one of the other counselors. Susie jumped a little when she saw Marie, then smiled. She shot a glance around to see if anyone was watching them. Not seeing Angela, she seemed satisfied.

Marie leaned in and indicated the cigarette. "This is new."

Susie shrugged. "Not new, just rare. Thought I needed one, you know?"

"I get it." A pause. "Can I have one?"

Susie smiled and grabbed the pack again. Soon, both of them were smoking and enjoying a silent moment together.

"This is dangerous," Susie said.

"What, smoking?" Marie said with a chuckle.

Susie joined her with a sweet chuckle of her own. "No, all this sneaking around. If these aren't accidents, then there's somebody killing people."

"You believe that?"

Susie nodded. "Yeah, I think that might be the case."

Marie pushed off the tree with one elbow and spun around to face Susie. "No killer can keep me away from you."

"Stop it," Susie said.

They kissed. It was a long, passionate kiss and Angela's eyebrows raised in surprise. *What are they doing?* It was hard to process what she was seeing. Susie and Marie were a couple. There was no other word for them—they were together. It made a certain amount of sense. Angela had seen them together often. Sometimes she had seen them holding hands, but she had thought that they were just friends.

But that clearly wasn't the case. She found herself thinking of her father. He and Lenny had been a couple, as well. Angela knew that it was out of the ordinary, at least when compared to most parents, but it had seemed natural. Sweet, even.

"Oh God," Susie said when the kiss broke. "You're trouble!" She chuckled. Shook her head. "But I can't resist you."

Marie cocked an eyebrow. "Ronnie has consolidated the cabins. I know an empty one nearby. Let's go. What do you say?"

Susie nodded. "Okay, let's do it."

The two women butted out their cigarettes on the tree and left together, holding hands. Angela watched them go. She had vague memories of her mother and father together but not many. She had been young when her mother had died, so her father and Lenny had been her whole world for a little while there. Before the accident. Before the death of the first Angela and her father. Before she had been made to put on the Angela mask.

She sighed and turned around, sitting on the soft earth and resting her back against a tree. She liked being a girl, hard though it may be, but becoming Angela had never sat well with her. Why couldn't she be her own kind of girl? Why didn't Aunt Martha allow her to be who she really was, a girl who had once been a boy but wasn't anymore?

What would her name be if she had been allowed to pick one? Penelope, maybe? She liked that one.

Smiling to herself, she was caught off guard by Paul, who grabbed her shoulder from behind and said, "Boo!"

Angela was startled, but not scared. Bullies were scary. Gender and sexual identity were scary. Paul was not—just infuriating sometimes.

"Better watch out," Paul said, "I could be the killer!"

Angela rolled her eyes. "You don't have it in you."

Paul rounded the tree and sat down beside her. "How do you know?"

She shrugged. "I just know, that's all."

He chuckled, waved a dismissive hand. "It's all bologna, anyway. I don't believe it."

"No?"

"No."

"So what do you think happened to Billy?" she asked, gnawing at her bottom lip.

"Somebody playing a prank that just got out of hand," he said, "that's all. Let's get outta here before someone catches us. I think I saw Susie and one of the other counselors a second ago."

She nodded and they both got up. Rushing to the lake, all of Angela's troubles melted away. The two of them ran on the beach like they didn't have a care in the world. It was a nice night out. There was a chill in the air, especially at the waterfront, but it wasn't cold. Paul playfully chased Angela around the boats and swimming equipment until he caught her. They wrapped their arms around each other, but before they could kiss, Angela snaked a leg around Paul's ankle, tripping the boy.

He tumbled to the ground, and she fell on top of him, both of them laughing. When the laughter stopped, they looked into each other's eyes, something silent but powerful passing between them. The kiss finally came—this one a real kiss. Angela tried to emulate Susie's kiss with Marie. Or the half-remembered times she had seen Lenny and her father kiss. And though she had no experience, she thought that Paul was a good kisser. Her, too.

Paul put both hands on her hips and rolled her over, getting on top of her. The kiss continued on unabated and Angela closed her eyes. It wasn't long before Paul was unbuttoning her shirt.

Angela's eyes snapped open. She was getting excited. Too excited. What if he saw? What if he noticed what was happening between her legs? What would he do if saw—if he *knew*? All at once, it was too much.

"Stop," she said, breaking the kiss.

"Come on," Paul said.

"I mean it—stop!"

He hesitated just long enough for her to escape from his grasp, getting up. Paul, looking confused and hurt, stood up as well. "Angela?"

"I'm sorry, Paul," she said.

Before he could say anything else, she turned and ran from him. She didn't stop until she had reached her own bunk. Having snuck out of the cabin, she made sure to be extra quiet when sneaking back in. Though Meg slept like a rock, she didn't want to risk her wrath. *I don't have to worry about Susie,* she thought with a smirk.

Trying to get her mind off Paul, she slinked into the cabin. The Other Angela was mercifully quiet so it was easy to sneak around without making a sound. Slipping through the main door, Angela proceeded inside. She took the extra precaution of dropping to her hands and knees and crawling once the door was shut behind her.

If anyone had been watching, they probably would have been afraid. Angela was a scary sight on all fours, stalking through the bunk in the darkness. Something out of the very worst nightmares.

Angela, herself, was aware of this—aware of how scary she was in this moment—and got a perverse thrill out of it. Deep down inside, the Other Angela was pleased. Angela could feel her smile in the pit of her stomach.

She sported an eerie smile of her own when she came face to face with a boy hiding near one of the beds.

The sudden presence of the boy—his name was Mozart, Angela recognized him—startled her and the Other Angela departed momentarily. She was a girl again and yelped in fear.

Mozart was also terrified and uttered a small cry of his own. Angela saw that he was clutching a pair of girl's underwear in one clenched fist. It was one of her's. Fear was replaced by anger in Angela's mind.

The other girls started to wake up, one by one, roused by the cries. Meg switched on the cabin light. Angela and Mozart popped up at the same moment, alongside three other boys. She also recognized these three: Clark, George and Bobby, the nasty boys who were making fun of her at the archery range and laughing at her during the water balloon incident. They were also clutching panties, sourced from all of the girl's cubicles.

"Panty raid!" Judy yelled from her bed.

That got all four boys moving. They darted out of the cabin, a hail of pillows raining down on them like a barrage of machine-gun fire.

"Get out, get out!" Meg shouted, managing to slap one of them in the back of the head as he disappeared through the door. The four of them were gone in seconds. Meg watched them go, shaking her head. "They're gonna hear about that tomorrow." She looked around, her gaze settled on Angela, and she frowned. Took a few steps towards the girl. Crossed her arms.

"Shoulda known you'd have something to do with this, Angela."

"I didn't do anything!" Angela said. She was heated, angry, and it came out as a shout. Meg instinctively took a step back.

"You were already awake," Meg shot back after recovering. "I bet you let them in. You wanted them to have your panties, didn't you?"

"You pervert," Judy said from the safety of her bed.

Meg poked Angela's chest with one too-long finger. "Mel's gonna hear about this. You hear me? *Mel.*" Shook her head. "Not your pal Ronnie," pointed at an empty bed, "not your girl-friend Susie. *Mel.*" She frowned, looking in the direction of her pointing finger. "Where is Susie?" Looked back at Angela.

Angela shrugged. "I don't know."

Meg looked confused for a moment, then she shook her head and the cruelty resurfaced. "Never mind. She's an adult, she can do what she wants. Everybody else back to bed!" Pointed back at Angela once again. "I'll talk to you after I speak with Mel tomorrow."

The girls collected their pillows and went back to bed. As Meg switched off the light, Angela climbed into her own bed. She hated Meg. The Other Angela was screaming inside her, telling her that they would get back at the counselor. Just you wait.

4

The next day—the last one, as it turned out—the counselors had decided on a game of capture the flag with the kids that remained. They had been separated into two teams, blue and white. Though the counselors had hyped the game up as large and elaborate, since it started it had devolved into a lot of running around the two flags set up at opposite ends of the large clearing near the archery range.

Paul—who was on the blue team—caught up with Angela —who was on the white team—shortly into the game. When he reached her, it looked like she had managed to give Ricky the slip. He had been sticking to her like glue the whole morning.

"Angela," he called after her. She looked back at him, looking not too sure of herself, but she stopped all the same, letting him catch up with her. "I still don't know why you were so upset about last night. I wasn't doing anything that bad, was I?"

"I'm sorry, Paul," she said. "I just wasn't ready." She looked away. "I just..." Trailing off.

"Hey, I understand." He reached out to put an arm around her. The moment his fingertips touched her shoulder, she flinched and pushed him away.

"Don't!" she said.

Paul shook his head. He didn't understand her at all. "What's the matter with you?"

"I have to go," she said.

With that, she left his side and disappeared into the woods. He watched her go, shaking his head.

"Girls," he said to himself.

"I don't know why you keep bothering with her."

Paul turned to see Judy approaching. She was just as beautiful as always, that mean look on her face.

"I mean," she said once she reached him, "she's so *small*."

"What do you know?" he said.

She sidled up beside him, her budding breasts touching his left shoulder. Instinctively, he looked down at her chest.

"I know a lot of things," she said. She touched the edge of his chin with a finger, lifted his head until he was looking her in the eye. "Want me to show you a few of them?"

Before he realized what he was doing, Paul was nodding. Emphatically.

5

Ricky caught up with Angela in the woods. He had been worried about her, of course, but didn't want to smother her. He always hated when his mom never gave him any privacy. Still, his mother hadn't been killing people—as far as he knew.

His grandfather had, though. He had heard stories, of course —rumors—but he was never sure if they had been true or not. The call with his mother had confirmed them, though. He had told his mother about the "accidents" at camp and his desire for her to come and pick them up. She had waffled, telling him that she was quite busy at the moment and that she didn't think that it would be possible but that she would try. That meant she wasn't coming.

They were on their own.

A part of him—a big part, if he was being honest—wanted to let Angela keep on doing what she had been doing. Her victims all deserved what they got, as far as he was concerned. But it was probably best if they just went home. He had his own troubles, of course. Ones that he didn't want to dwell on.

But since they were apparently stuck here, he was determined to maintain some kind of normalcy. They would play campground games, tell stories, eat junk food—if he was ever allowed back at the canteen—and have fun. He would protect Angela, of course, but he would make sure that she had fun, too. He wanted her to be normal—or as normal as possible given the circumstances.

"Angela," he said when he caught up to her, "you gotta help me. I got a great plan to get the flag." She looked at him without much enthusiasm. "We cut through the woods here." He gestured around them. "Sneak up behind them! You go in one way and I go in the other. It can't miss!"

"I don't feel like playing, Ricky," Angela said.

"Oh, come on. Help me out, will you? I can't do it by myself. Please?" She didn't look convinced. Trying to come up with another angle, he searched his brain. Came up with what seemed like a brilliant strategy. "After we get the flag the game will be over and you won't have to play anymore. Okay?"

Finally, she sighed and nodded. "Alright, where do we have to go?"

"Follow me."

They turned around and headed back the direction Angela had come. A minute later, Ricky pointed through the thick trees. "The flag should be around there, past the trees." He pointed in another direction. "You go in from this side, and I'll walk around and attack from the other side. They'll never be able to catch both of us."

"How do I know when to come out?" Angela asked.

"Good question. Tell you what. Give me about five minutes, and when I see them run after you, I'll sneak out and grab the flag."

She shook her head. "I hope it works, because I don't want to be out here anymore."

"No sweat," he said, "it's foolproof."

She went off to sneak through the woods. Ricky watched her go. Movement on the ground between them caught his attention. Looking down, he saw a small snake slither through the undergrowth. He frowned. It was probably harmless. Most of the snakes around here were. Water snakes, garden snakes—the usual variety.

After taking a moment to shoo it away, just in case, he went off to get into position himself. Hearing conversation somewhere nearby, he ducked down so as not to be caught by the other team. He creeped through the woods as quietly as he could manage until he saw two figures.

It was Paul and Judy. They were standing quite close to each other.

"Come on," Judy said, "no one will see us."

They kissed. Ricky looked on, shaking his head. But damn, did Judy look good! Ricky adjusted his crotch and shifted his stance.

"Jesus," Judy said as the kiss broke, "will you loosen up already?"

Paul nodded and they kissed again. This one was better. Longer. The boy really looked like he was getting into it.

"There," Judy said when this second kiss broke, "that wasn't so bad, was it?"

"I guess not," Paul said.

From Ricky's vantage point, he could see that Paul had a hard-on as he went in for another kiss. This time, Paul reached around and grabbed Judy's ass as they kissed. She, in turn, put a hand on his crotch.

Just as it was getting exciting, Ricky saw his cousin lingering nearby, also watching the new couple. "Shit," he whispered to himself. Angela walked towards Judy and Paul, and the two of them turned to regard her. For a brief moment, everyone was frozen in place, no one wanting to make the first move.

Then Angela turned and stalked away. Paul broke off from Judy and went after her.

"Angela!" he called after her.

"Hey," Judy said as he left, "where are you going?!"

There was no reason to hide anymore, so Ricky stepped out

into plain view and shook his head as he approached Judy. "You're a real scumbag, Judy, you know that?"

"Fuck you, Ricky," she said to him as he passed. "You're just jealous."

It was true, and that's what hurt the most. Not that Paul was stepping out on his cousin. No, it was because he wanted Judy for himself.

"Same to you," he said, not looking at her, but flipping her the bird behind his back as he left the woods.

They ended up losing the game.

6

After Capture The Flag, it was time for swim period. As usual, Angela sat on the bleachers by herself as most of the other kids splashed about in the water. She watched them with a weary eye. Her mind was elsewhere. She was thinking of what had happened on that lake when she was a child, all those years ago. In another life.

Paul came strutting out of the water, grabbing a beach towel on his way out and draping it over his shoulders. Angela made a point of not looking at him, even when he reached her and stood by her side.

"Mind if I sit here?" he asked.

She didn't answer. He sighed and sat down beside her anyway. For a moment, he was silent, fiddling with his towel, using it to dry his hair. After another sigh, he spoke up. "Angela, I'm really sorry about what happened before. I really am." He rested his elbows on his knees and looked out at the water, matching her posture. "I don't know what happened. She just wouldn't leave me alone."

Apparently finding the water too boring, he turned to regard her. "Come on, Angela! Please? Give me another chance, will you? *Please?*"

She said nothing. Inside, the Other Angela was fuming.

Angela could picture her, a caged beast rattling the bars of its prison, testing it for weaknesses. Pleading with Angela to let her out.

When Judy appeared, she startled both of them, walking up to them silently and speaking before they had a chance to see her. "Back together so soon?"

Her smile was wider and meaner than ever. Today she wore a two-piece swimsuit that looked too small for her body. Neither of them answered her, of course.

"Boy, Angela," she continued, "you sure are forgiving." She licked her bottom lip as if she were tasting the residue of Paul's kiss. "Especially after he told me what a prude you are."

Paul looked up at her, eyes wide. Judy smiled down at him.

"That is the word you used," she said, "isn't it, Paul?"

Angela looked at him and knew at once that it was true. He *had* said that about her. He didn't even look at her before whispering, "I gotta go," getting up from the bleachers and leaving.

He's leaving again! Angela thought. *He's leaving me alone with her. Why is he doing that* again?

Once he was gone, Judy sat down next to Angela. She sighed, put a hand on Angela's knee. Looked pointedly at her. "Just us girls now. It's really no big deal, you know. I mean, he's okay for you." Her eyes widened with inspiration. "I know what'll cheer you up! How about a little swim? What do you say we get that beautiful bod of yours into the water, hmm?"

Angela shook her head. She couldn't go in the water. Even though many of the kids had left, there were still too many of them in the water and on the beach. They might figure out her secret!

"Oh, what's the matter?" Judy said. "You afraid?"

Angela shut down completely, staring off towards the water again. The Other Angela screamed inside her.

"Huh?" Judy prompted. Her smile disappeared when Angela refused to answer. She stood up. "Well say something, you spoiled little bitch!"

Meg appeared seemingly out of nowhere, leaned on her pal Judy, and looked at Angela like she was some ugly specimen in a petri dish. "What's the problem?"

"My good friend Angela here doesn't feel like going in the water today," Judy said.

"Oh, she doesn't, does she?" Meg said, her smile just as mean as Judy's. "Well, I think we can fix that."

Before Angela had a chance to do anything, Meg grabbed her by the waist and picked her up. She was far bigger than Angela and slung her over a shoulder with ease. Angela batted at the counselor's back and kicked out with her feet, but it didn't do any good. They were already halfway to the water.

7

Ricky came out of the water, raking back his wet hair with both hands. As he sauntered onto the shore looking for his cousin, Mel approached him. The camp owner had a cigar with him, of course, and he took it out of his mouth to speak. "Hello, Ricky."

"Hey, Mel," Ricky said, distracted. Someone was next to Angela, but he couldn't quite make out who it was. There was still water in his eyes.

"Seems we haven't had much of a chance to talk," Mel said. "How's your summer been so far?"

Don't give anything away, he thought. "All right, I guess," he said.

"Just all right?"

"Well, it would have been better if there were more guys around. It's kind of hard to get a ball game up now, you know?"

"Yeah," Mel said, sticking the cigar back in his mouth. He spoke around it. "It is a shame so many had to leave. With all this bad publicity, I don't see how I can hold onto the camp—"

"No!" Angela cried out. "Put me down!"

Ricky turned and saw Meg carrying Angela out to the water. *That bitch!* He had to stop her, had to save his cousin.

"One sec," he said to Mel, and made to leave. Mel caught him by the wrist and held fast. Though he looked old and frail, he was surprisingly strong. Ricky looked up at him. "What are you doing?" he shouted.

"Just like all the other times," Mel said and actually spit out his cigar. It landed in the sand at his feet. "She gets into trouble and you run to her rescue." His grip on Ricky's wrist tightened. "You try to take care of everybody. How you gonna do it this time? Another drowning, or something worse?"

Real fear shuddered through him. It must have shown on his face. "What are you talking about? Let me go!"

"I saw you those times!" Mel shouted in his face. "In the rec hall, the water balloon, you killed them!"

"Don't throw me in the water!" Angela cried out. Meg had just reached the dock.

Ricky struggled, but couldn't break Mel's grip. His wrist was turning red.

"You killed them to destroy me, didn't you?" Mel said. "Didn't you?!"

"No!" Angela cried out as Meg tossed her into the water. Judy was close behind them, laughing as Angela flailed about in the water.

Ronnie rushed over to Mel and grabbed him by the shoulder. "Jesus Christ, Mel! What the hell are you doing?"

The camp owner let go of Ricky. The boy ran towards the water and his cousin. Hal, the lifeguard, approached from the dock. With his help, Ricky, angry and cussing, managed to get Angela out of the water. His cousin looked humiliated. She clutched her crotch and looked around at everyone who was watching.

Meg and Judy leered at them. Judy was laughing. Meg's arms were crossed and she leaned over to speak to them. "Oh, poor baby."

"You're a real peckerhead, you know that, Meg?" Hal said.

Ricky led Angela away from the water towards the bleachers. Along the way, Mozart and a group of younger boys building a castle kicked sand at Angela. Ricky grabbed one of their plastic buckets and tossed it at them. "Little fuckers!"

"Hey!" Hal shouted at the group from the dock. "Animals! Knock it off!"

Mozart and the boys doubled over with laughter. Ricky ignored them and helped Angela to the bleachers. They sat down. Ricky grabbed a towel that was hanging over the side of one of the benches and draped it around Angela. She clung to it like a baby.

"Calm down, Angela," he said. "It's okay now. Everything's gonna be alright."

Ricky watched Meg and Judy leave the dock. They were terrible. Both of them. He shot daggers at Judy. She was so gorgeous. Even now, he still wanted her. Desired her.

But she wouldn't have him.

"We won't let them get away with this, that's for sure," he whispered to Angela. "I promise we won't."

CHAPTER
EIGHT

A RELAXING SHOWER

1

"All right, everybody here?" Ronnie asked, clipboard in hand. "Okay, there's not much on the roster tonight."

It was already past dark, and Susie stood with her fellow, remaining counselors near Ronnie's shack. They had already lost three. Susie was considering leaving herself, but she wasn't going to leave Marie at camp all alone. They stood next to each other, Meg nearby. Mel stayed back, near the door to Ronnie's shack, letting his head counselor do his job.

"After dinner, we got the social in the rec hall, of course," Ronnie continued. "Piece of cake. We're looking at a pretty small group, so that won't take long. Those on duty can start bringing your kids up around nine."

"Let's hope nobody gets murdered before then," Eddie, one of the counselors, quipped. There was scattered laughter, Meg among them. Susie frowned.

"Pipe down," Ronnie said. "You won't be taking your charges to the social. I got bigger and better things planned for you tonight, Eddie."

"A night off?" Eddie said, spreading his arms wide.

"Even better. You're gonna take those little darlings of yours on a camping trip on the lake. Campfire, ghost stories, sleeping under the stars, bacon and eggs for breakfast. The works."

Eddie frowned. "I can't wait."

"Okay," Ronnie said, "as for the rest of you, you're all on duty except for… Jerry and Meg. And that's it."

"Anybody want to switch?" Eddie said. There were no takers.

As everyone dispersed, Susie and Marie lingered near Meg, who looked elated. Ronnie was speaking with Mel, going over various camp issues.

"Lucky," Marie said to Meg.

"You ain't kidding," Meg said.

"I sure could use a night off," Marie said.

"We all could," Susie said.

Meg dropped them a salute. "See you tomorrow, girls!"

She headed towards Mel just as Ronnie left his side. Got real close to the camp owner. He had just produced a new cigar and Meg plucked it out of his hand and stuck it between her lips playfully.

"Guess who's got the night off?"

"Congratulations," Mel said.

"About that dinner you promised me. You know, at your place? What do you think?"

Mel looked her up and down. "Yeah… Nine, nine-thirty?"

"You got it. See you then!"

She took the cigar out of her mouth and stuck it into his. With that, she left, shooting Susie and Marie a wicked smile as she did. Susie watched her go, shaking her head. The two of them started back towards their bunks. When no one else was around, they linked hands.

"You don't approve of Mel and Meg?" Marie asked.

Susie shrugged. "I don't know. He's so much older than her."

"Yeah?"

"And he's her boss. That just doesn't seem right."

Marie nodded. "I understand. But at least they don't feel ashamed to be seen together."

Susie sighed. "Fair enough."

"Do you really think it would be so bad? People knowing about us?"

"My mom would kill me."

"You really care what your mom thinks?"

Susie had been raised to obey her parents. It had been a strict upbringing—Catholic and oppressive. So she gave Marie's question some real thought before answering. "I guess the short answer is yes, I do care."

"But?" Marie prompted.

"But I shouldn't."

"Now you're starting to get it."

Marie leaned in for a kiss and Susie managed to keep from looking around before accepting it. It was a good one.

2

Eddie was getting his "little darlings," as Ronnie called them, together. His bunk now housed all of the younger boys, which—by this time—only consisted of five rowdy kids. Three of them were real brats: Clark, George, and Bobby. Eddie figured that their parents didn't want them home from camp early, or possibly didn't even mind if they were murdered up here.

In fact, where are they right now? he thought, looking around. When he heard firecrackers outside, he had his answer. Sticking his head out the door, he called the troublemakers inside. As the three of them rounded their way into the bunk, Eddie saw Mozart trying to slink away.

"Mozart," he called out, "get over here!" The boy trudged over to him. "You know better than to encourage them. Don't you?"

"I don't know," Mozart said, eyes downtrodden.

"You don't know?" Eddie shook his head. "Tell you what, I'm taking these amazing kids out camping tonight. You're gonna come with me to supervise them. Maybe then you'll 'know.' How's that sound?"

"What?" Mozart said, gesturing to the small number of kids assembled in the bunk. "There's like five of them! You don't need my help supervising them. Besides, I was going to the social."

"Not anymore, you're not. Get in here."

Mozart sighed and proceeded inside. He looked around like he was lost.

"Come on," Eddie said, "help 'em pack."

Mozart looked at him like a drowned puppy.

"Get to it!" Eddie said.

Finally, after another minute of hesitation and complaining, Mozart got to it.

3

Meg sauntered into her bunk like she was a celebrity. Judy had just taken a shower after dinner and was getting ready for the social, blow-drying her hair. Most of the other girls were getting ready, too. Judy looked at Angela, who was sitting on her bed nearby, with narrowed eyes.

Is she going to the social wearing that? she thought. *And isn't she going to take a shower?*

Judy shook her head. The girl was hopeless. She would never be able to keep a boy around and interested. It was kind of sad in a way.

Meg grabbed a towel, shampoo + conditioner, and a toothbrush from her cubicle. Judy smiled at the counselor, who smiled back. Now, Meg, on the other hand, would always keep men around and interested. She knew what she was doing and Judy admired that.

"What are you so happy about?" Judy asked.

"I got a date tonight," Meg said, raising her eyebrows twice in quick succession for emphasis.

"Oh, yeah? With who?"

Meg smirked. "I think you know who."

Judy knew. Mel. He was old and gross, but he was a powerful person, at least around here, so Judy understood the appeal. She may not have wanted to touch the guy with a ten-foot pole herself, but she understood all the same.

Meg walked into the back, presumably to take a shower. Judy smiled to herself, anticipating what was about to happen. Sure enough, a moment later Meg emerged from the back. There was already a line of girls waiting to take a shower. And Meg didn't want to keep her extremely old paramour waiting, now did she?

"Judy," Meg said, "do you know if the water is still on next door?"

"I think so," Judy said with a nod.

"Great. See you later."

Judy waved goodbye to her friend. As Meg left, Judy saw that Angela was looking at the counselor as the older girl disappeared through the door.

"Bet you don't need a costume for Halloween, do you, Angela?" she said. "You just have to be yourself to scare people."

Too bad there wasn't anybody around to hear that one. It surely would have gotten some

laughs. Angela didn't answer. She got up from her bed and headed towards the door. *I guess she is wearing that to the social,* Judy thought.

"You're wrong, Judy," Angela said, standing in the doorway. "I do dress up sometimes."

"Oh, yeah? As what?"

Angela flashed her eyes wide for a second before answering, "The Horned Serpent." She smiled and it was *hideous*. Judy found herself shrinking deeper into her bed. After a moment, Angela was gone, through the door and out into the night.

4

Judy had been right: the water was still on in the cabin next door. Since Meg still had some time, she decided to take a long shower. She wanted to really scrub and soak those pores. Take her time. It was relaxing, which was just what she needed right now. After the shower, she had a couple fat lines of coke waiting for her.

The shower stalls at Camp Arawak weren't exactly luxurious. They were basically boxy rectangles made of lacquered plywood on three sides, a hanging plastic curtain on the fourth, tile on the floor and nothing on top. The plywood couldn't have been more than an inch thick at the most. The camp wasn't exactly the most well-maintained or sanitary place around, but Mel tried his best to keep it all together.

Seeing the way that Judy acted when Meg told her about her relationship with Mel, she figured that most people thought that it was some kind of angle, or a deception somehow. The reality was that Meg simply liked Mel. He was funny, and sort of intense sometimes. Meg wasn't the kind of girl to self-analyze, but her attachment to Mel might have had something to do with never having a real male parental figure around. Her father had left when she had been less than two years old, and her mother never found anyone steady to stick around. Since she had no uncles, or grandparents, Meg tended to gravitate towards teachers, authority figures, and, of course, counselors here at Camp Arawak when she was younger. So it felt natural to her that she would be attracted to someone like Mel.

Meg was deep in her thoughts, her arms working soap into her body robotically, when the lights went out in the cabin. For a second, she thought it might be some kind of power failure, but that was silly. It was obviously someone messing with her. Someone playing a prank.

"Who's there?" she called out.

There was no answer, but she could hear someone moving around. Listening carefully, she tried to follow the sound, but it was no good. Whoever it was, they could be silent when they wanted to.

Meg, despite her age, despite her authority, was still a child. And children are afraid of the dark. Suddenly, she felt very vulnerable—exposed. A shower in the dark was something out of a nightmare. She backed into one of the thin plywood walls of the stall, felt her weight bowing it. It didn't exactly inspire confidence.

Slowly, the heat of the shower disappeared to be replaced by cold water. Meg's teeth chattered. She closed her arms across her chest. Dropped the bar of soap she had been clutching.

The sound of someone running towards her—from behind— made every hair on her body stand out. *But I'm up against a wall! I'm safe!*

This illusion was shattered when something sharp and painful plunged through the plywood and penetrated her back. It embedded itself between two ribs, puncturing a lung. Meg felt every bit of air leave her body in a rush. She tried to draw breath but all she got was pain.

But if she didn't move—if she didn't get out of the shower right now—then she was going to die. She had to force herself off the wall and whatever she was stuck to.

With a mighty effort, she pushed off the wall. She uttered a single, strained, painful cry as the edge of the knife came out of her back. A spray of blood splattered the wall. Meg whirled towards the heavy-duty plastic shower curtain and stumbled, slipped. The pain was too much to keep a proper balance. She put out a hand to brace herself and landed the very center of her palm on the point of the knife sticking out of the wall.

It went right through her hand and Meg screamed a silent

scream. Blood bubbled out of the wound and ran down the wall. Before she had a chance to make a move—any kind of move—the knife was suddenly gone, leaving only pain in its wake.

Meg tried to move again as the sound of running feet rounded the shower. Whoever it was, they were going to come through the shower curtain. She opened her mouth to scream, but no sound emerged from it. Her lungs were aching for air.

The shower curtain parted and a leering, wide-eyed nightmare came into the shower.

Meg didn't know who it was. It was simply a shape, a boogeyman crawling out of the deepest pit of childhood terror. Then she realized that it was Angela. Angela, her eyes now impossibly large. Her face split with a razor blade smile.

She held a hunting knife stained with blood—Meg's blood. It was the last thing that Meg ever saw. Its blade glinted in the water as it came down towards her. Into her. Again. And again.

And again.

5

When the Other Angela was finally finished, and Meg's badly mutilated body lay on the floor of the shower, Angela stood over it, head cocked to one side like a Cocker Spaniel. For a moment, she didn't understand what she was seeing. When she finally got the picture, she nodded. *Okay, that's done.*

Calmly, she stepped out of the shower and examined herself. She was covered in blood. That was no good. She would have to get cleaned up.

She looked down at Meg's dead body and considered moving it. But only for a moment. It didn't really bother her. Stepping into the shower, she stood over the body and under the shower head.

The cold didn't bother her, either. It was rather refreshing, actually. Relaxing, even. She smiled.

Turning around to make sure the water washed away all the blood, Angela was careful not to trip over Meg's body. It was kind of funny, actually. She chuckled as she danced around the corpse.

Inside, the Other Angela joined her.

6

Paul wasn't enjoying the social at all. It was bad enough that dinner was terrible—an attempt at sloppy joes that could only be described as a crime against humanity—now there was this horrible gathering of a dwindling group of sad-looking kids.

He hadn't seen Angela yet, but there had been plenty of Judy to go around. She spent most of her time with Mike, laughing at all of his jokes, no matter how bad they were. Paul watched her from afar. She was still extremely desirable to him, but he hated her all the same, especially because she no longer seemed interested in him. Having humiliated him in front of Angela, her mission was apparently accomplished.

Paul sat by himself, joylessly enjoying a PowerHouse candy bar, when he saw Angela enter the rec room. Perking up, he tossed what remained of the candy bar into a nearby trash can and got up, heading towards Angela.

"Hi," he said when he reached her.

Angela took one look at him and turned around to leave the rec hall. Paul followed her outside. "Hey, wait. Don't act like that."

On the steps leading out of the rec hall, she finally stopped. Sighed and turned to him. "Do you know where Ricky is?"

"He's back at the bunk lying down," Paul said. "Said he didn't feel well after dinner, but that he might stop by later."

She nodded and started to leave once again. Paul stopped her, grabbing her shoulder. "Look, I'm sorry about how I acted earlier. Can't you forgive me? Please?"

She said nothing, just looked at him, her usual blank expression on her face. Paul placed his other hand on her and met her gaze.

"I was a jerk, okay?" he said.

Still nothing. He thought about giving up at that moment, just turning and leaving, but right then the doors to the rec hall opened up and Judy and Mike came stumbling out. Paul saw Mike slip what looked like a small flask into his back pocket.

"Excuse us, kids," Judy said, pushing past Paul and Angela. She smiled meanly at them, then said to Mike, "Don't they make a lovely couple?" They both laughed loud as they disappeared into the night.

Paul watched them go and shook his head. He suddenly felt reinvigorated and turned back to Angela. "She's a real bitch."

Angela nodded slowly.

"Look," Paul said, "one more chance. Last chance?"

She struggled out of his grip—*She's stronger than she looks*—and turned away from him. Paul felt the deep sting of defeat before she spoke up, not looking at him.

"Meet me at the waterfront after the social," she said.

A big smile spread across his lips. "All right! I'll be there."

It worked. He had one last chance. And he didn't intend to blow it.

CHAPTER
NINE

THE HORNED SERPENT

1

Mozart was having trouble sleeping. Camping out under the stars may have been appealing to some, but it held no interest for him. Plus, it was unseasonably cold. A strong breeze wafted in from the lake and into the woods where Eddie and the others had set up camp, chilling them. Now they were supposed to be sleeping, but Mozart doubted any of them were.

Sure enough, one of the little brats piped up, "Eddie, I'm cold."

"Go to sleep," Eddie murmured. "Once you're asleep you won't be cold."

"But I'm *cold*," the child insisted. A few of the others roused from their sleeping bags and looked at Eddie. Clark and Bobby appeared to be passed out, but the others, George included, were awake.

"I wanna go back to my bunk," the cold kid said.

"I wanna go back, too," another said.

Eddie sat up, rubbed sleep out of his eyes—he must have been sleeping fine, Mozart thought—and looked around.

George had gotten partially out of his sleeping bag and was fiddling with the hand axe they had brought with them.

"Don't do that," Eddie said. "That's not a toy, you know."

George snatched his hand away from the axe, shot Eddie a mischievous smile. Eddie shook his head, looked at Mozart.

"You're all right to keep an eye on the others while I take these two back?" he asked.

Mozart sighed, but he nodded.

"Alright," Eddie said, looking at the other two brats. "Pack up your stuff and let's go." He looked at George. "I want you back in your bag, eyes shut. You better be sleeping like the dead when I get back. Understand?"

George nodded and crawled back into his bag. Mozart did the same. As Eddie and the two brats packed up and left—the only kids being Clark, Bobby and George now—Mozart finally, slowly drifted to sleep.

He couldn't have been down more than fifteen minutes before he was awoken once again, this time by a soft hand on his cheek. It took him a few seconds to get his eyes open, a moment to return to the waking world. When he finally came around, he saw a face very close to his own looking down at him. He frowned.

It was Angela.

Her eyes were wide and large, and she had a strange expression on her face that Mozart hadn't ever seen before. It was a little scary, but it was her nonetheless. What was she doing out here?

She smiled down at him. He opened his mouth to speak, but she quickly shushed him with a finger to her lips. Still smiling wide, she straddled him. *What's she doing?* he thought. *Oh shit, is this really happening?* He shot a look at the three younger boys. They all seemed to be asleep. He looked back at Angela, his prick stiffening in his pants.

Still smiling, Angela raised her free hand from behind her back. She was holding something. It took Mozart a second—too long, as it turned out—to figure out what it was: *his own hunting knife.* Angela dragged it across his throat in one swift motion, slitting him open from ear to ear.

Shock came before pain. He must be having a nightmare. A strange, horrible nightmare. This couldn't be happening. What did he do to deserve this?

As the pain finally hit him, and blood erupted from the wound and bubbled out of his mouth, Mozart looked into the girl's terrifying eyes and saw the reason. The panty raid. The sand kicked at her by the lake. The mean laughter. He had become a bully with the younger boys to escape bullying himself. Now he was paying for it.

Angela stepped off him, a knee planted in Mozart's stomach as she moved, and stood up. Mozart grabbed at his throat, instantly soaking his hands in his own blood. *There's so much of it!* Angela calmly retrieved the hand axe from a nearby tree stump. She stood over George.

She brought it down on the boy's forehead, splitting his head in two with one, hard swing. There was a hideous crunch as George's skull gave way. The boy twitched only once.

Angela proceeded to Bobby and buried the axe again and again in the boy's chest. Bobby gasped once and convulsed. After the fourth strike, he was dead. It was a slaughterhouse at her feet.

Finally, Angela stepped over Clark. She looked at Mozart. Frantically, he shook his head and reached out with a blood-soaked hand, tried to plead with her, but he couldn't make any sounds. Blood cascaded out of his neck, and he could feel the world getter smaller.

Angela brought the axe down on Clark's left leg. The boy screamed in pain. The limb was severed. Mozart could see it through the slash in the sleeping bag now, a stump of an upper thigh spurting blood into the cool night air. As Clark sat up in terror, Angela struck again, chopping off the boy's left arm. It hit the ground and rolled into the dying campfire, where it started to cook, stoking the flames. Clark's scream cut short when Angela brought the axe down where Clark's shoulder met his neck.

Clark's head lolled to one side. When Angela pulled the axe out it went swinging in the other direction. His body dropped to the ground as Angela stepped towards Mozart once again.

Mozart shook his head in panic. Each movement generated another shot of horrible pain. Angela remained unmoved, and she raised the axe high above her head. She brought it down on Mozart's outstretched hand, bisecting it between his pointer and middle finger and continuing down into his wrist. A twist and she pulled it out with a squelch. When she brought it down again, she hit him square in the chin. His jaw split in two along with his tongue.

Mozart made a few pained gurgling sounds before life finally departed him.

2

"Did you hear that?" Mike said, breaking the kiss.

He and Judy were alone in her bunk. The only light was from an open window. The kiss had been good, but a little wet for her liking. Maybe it had something to do with the vodka from Mike's flask they had both been sharing.

"What?" she said, annoyed.

"Sounded like a scream," Mike said.

Judy shook her head. "I didn't hear anything." In fact, she *had* heard what sounded like distant screams, she just didn't care. She grabbed the back of his head, said, "Come on," and brought him in for another kiss.

This one lasted a little longer, and was a little better, so Judy was especially disappointed when Mike began to choke and cough into her mouth. She broke the kiss and looked at him with contempt. There was a tear running down one of his cheeks.

"Oh, for Christ's sake," she said.

"Sorry," Mike said and wiped the tear away. He produced his flask and took a quick swig.

"You're still thinking about your stupid dead friends, aren't you?" Judy said.

Mike didn't answer for a moment, but Judy could see that his eyes were wet and threatening to leak. She knew she was right.

"Can't you just be a man?" she said.

He nodded, wiped away another tear just as it formed. Just when he got it together, Judy heard someone coming towards the bunk. She looked at Mike. "Quick, under the bed!"

Scrambling, Mike dropped down. His big frame barely fit, so Judy crossed her fingers that this would work. She grabbed a magazine and laid on her stomach, opened the magazine to a random page and pretended like she was reading.

The door to the bunk opened and Mel came in. *Shit*, Judy thought, *we're screwed now*.

"Hey, Judy," Mel said.

"Hi, Mel," Judy said.

"Not going to the social?"

"I already went, but I was a little tired. Thought I'd call it an early night."

"Have you seen Meg?" Mel asked.

"Not in a while," Judy said. "You looking for her?"

He nodded. Rubbed at his mouth. To Judy, it looked like a nervous tick. *Where's his cigar?* she wondered.

"Yeah," he said.

"She's not at the social?"

"No. Susie says that she never showed up. When was the last time you saw her?"

"She went next door to take a shower, I think."

He looked angry, frustrated. "*When?*"

"I don't know," Judy said. "Sometime after dinner."

"Alright. Thank you." He made for the door. Turned back

around. "You know you shouldn't read in the dark. It's bad for your eyes."

Fuck you, she thought, but flashed him a smile. Finally, he was gone. Mike crawled out from under the bed a second later.

"I better get going before we get caught," he said.

"What?" Judy said, shocked. "You just got here!"

Mike indicated the door. "That was too close."

"He's not gonna come back, and you know it."

He stood up from the bed. Shrugged. "You never know." Turned to leave. "See you tomorrow."

"Don't bet on it," Judy said. Just before he reached the door, Judy gave him one final goodbye. "Chickenshit crybaby."

He only hesitated for a moment, shook his head, opened the door and left, taking a short moment to see if anyone was around before disappearing into the night. Judy was left alone once more. She put the magazine aside and grabbed her curling iron. Maybe there were some other boys heading back to their bunks from the social who still wanted to party. If that was the case, then she better make sure her hair looked good.

3

As Mike left Judy for the last time, Mel stood in the cabin next door. There was a light on in the back. He could also hear the shower running.

How long does a shower take? He shook his head and proceeded into the back. Meg probably had some task that she needed to take care of first before getting ready. In fact, he had a few tasks of his own, one of which was having a few drinks to calm his nerves. Still, she was an hour late, which wasn't like her.

Maybe we'll just have a nice little time right here. He walked towards the shower stall as quietly as he could, intending to scare her. Then maybe join her. A hot shower sounded good right about now, especially with some company.

Creeping up on the shower stall, he pulled aside the plastic curtain, uttering a pathetic, "Boo!" He frowned when he found the shower empty. The water was still running, but there wasn't anyone here. On one of the walls he saw a hole and a spray of blood. "Jesus."

Closing the curtain, he turned around. *Was it some kind of prank?* No, he didn't think so. This was serious. He left the bathroom and went into the main area of the bunk once more, this time fiddling around in the dark for a light switch. He finally found one near one of the cubicles.

When he flicked it on, it took him a minute to figure out what he was looking at. Meg's face stared back at him from the cubicle over the bed, eyes wide, mouth hanging open.

When realization struck, he stumbled back and nearly fell over. Meg had been cut into several pieces and stuffed into the cubicle. Her legs were stacked on top of each other on one shelf. On another, her torso had been crammed in, bowing the shelves above and below it. Her decapitated head was the centerpiece, arranged in front of her severed, crossed arms, and looking sightlessly out at Mel.

"No," he moaned. "Not you, Meg. Not you, too!"

He covered his face as if that would wipe away the reality of what he was seeing. *It's that son-of-a-bitch*, he thought. *He did this! Ricky Fucking Thomas!*

Clawing his fingers down his face and leaving marks, he bit his lower lip in rage, drawing blood. "I'll get him, Meg," he told her dead body. "He's not gonna get away with this!"

Murder on his mind, Mel ran from the cabin in search of Ricky Thomas.

4

Judy had the radio on as she curled her hair. Deep Purple was playing, "Hush." There was something sinister about it and, even though it was old, Judy felt that it had real power. She smiled as she listened to it. The light was off—she knew where every strand of hair on her head lay so had no need of it.

The Beatles came on after that and Judy sighed, rolled her eyes. Reaching over with her free hand, she changed the station to something modern. She found Blue Oyster Cult—"Joan Crawford"—and left it there. This was a good one, too. If "Hush" was sinister, then this one was on an entirely different level.

She continued curling her hair as Blue Oyster Cult went on describing apocalyptic scenes of evocative carnage. After a while, it was too much. Judy was actually starting to get scared here in the dark, in a cabin out in the middle of the woods. As the titular Joan was telling Christina that mother was home, Judy reached out and switched off the radio. She shuddered. That was enough of that.

She was almost done curling her hair when the door to the bunk swung open. Judy looked up from what she was doing and saw someone standing in the doorway. They were backlit, and she couldn't make them out.

"Mike?" she said. "Is that you? Who is that?" When there was no answer forthcoming, she sighed. "Well, don't turn the light on, then we'll have to go to the stupid social."

Whoever it was closed the door behind them and proceeded inside. Judy put the curling iron aside and grabbed a brush to attend to her hair.

"See any cute boys on your way back?" she asked. "I was thinking about sneaking out. Wanna come, too?"

The figure had reached her bed, stood uncomfortably close, and Judy frowned, reeling back. "Hey, give me some space, why don't you?!"

As her eyes adjusted to the dark, the figure's face came into focus. "Oh, it's you." All contempt. "What do you want?"

Ricky Thomas didn't respond. Didn't say anything at all. He only struck out with a fist and hit her across the face. Judy fell onto her bed, blood gushing from her nose. She tried to fight back, putting up a hand, but Ricky batted it away, grabbing her wrist and twisting it to one side. It wasn't broken, but it hurt all the same.

As she tried to sit up, Ricky punched her again, this time in the left eye. This hit was even harder, and Judy's eyesight went all bright white for a moment. She fell back onto her pillow once again. Ricky wrapped his left hand around her throat and squeezed.

"Pick on my cousin?" he whispered. "Bully her? I'll show you."

He squeezed tighter and Judy couldn't breathe. She grasped at Ricky's hand, but it was no good. His grip was too tight.

"Don't wanna spend any time with me anymore?!" Ricky shouted.

He grabbed the curling iron with his free hand and forced her legs apart with his knees.

Oh God, where's he going with that? she thought. Ricky plunged the steaming hot iron between her legs. The pain was incredible. She wanted to breathe but couldn't. Wanted to scream but it was useless.

She batted at Ricky's arms, tried to kick with her legs, but all the strength was leaving her body. *I'm dying. Oh God, I'm gonna die right here, right now.* Tears ran down her cheeks. In those last, horrible moments, she was just a scared little girl.

She looked up into Ricky's horrible face as the world closed in around it. Black bugs crawled in at the edges of her vision. It only took a minute or two longer for her to die, but it felt like forever.

5

Eddie yawned as he returned to the little campground. The two cold campers had been successfully delivered to Gene's bunk, where they would spend the night with some of the older boys. Mission accomplished.

All he wanted to do now was crawl into his sleeping bag and hit the hay. It would be cold, it would be uncomfortable, but it would be rest just the same.

As he approached the little camp, he could smell cooking meat. *What the hell is that? Pork? Chicken, maybe?*

Chicken? He shook his head. That didn't make any sense. They did have bacon for the morning. Did the little brats get hungry and decide to have a cookout? He sighed.

"All right, you troublemakers," he said as he entered the clearing where they had set up camp, "if you're cooking up that bacon now, then there won't be any for the morning."

What he saw made him stop cold.

Mozart and the three young campers had been chopped apart. Their sleeping bags had been slashed and at least one of the kids had been cut into several pieces. An arm—Clark's— was sitting in the fire, cooking. That was what he had smelled.

"Oh God," he said. "Jesus Christ."

He tried to stop himself from vomiting and lost. Leaning over, hands on his knees, dinner came cascading out of him, splashing onto the lush forest ground. He dropped to his knees, vomit, snot, and tears spouting from his face. It was the single worst moment of his life. He kept thinking of the kids' parents. What would they tell them?

Thoughts of who had committed the murders never even entered his mind.

6

Mike took another swig from his flask and stumbled ahead. Leaving Judy, he had wandered into the woods with no particular destination in mind. All he wanted to do was drink himself silly and remember his dead friends.

The moon was high above him, and the sky was full of stars. Mike looked up and felt the enormity of it all. Saw the world and all the people on it for what they truly were: nothing. It was all meaningless. What did it matter who lived and died, what anyone did in any particular moment? Their lives were all nothing in the grand scheme of things.

Mike had never had these kinds of thoughts before. He wasn't what anyone would describe as a deep thinker. But the deaths of Billy and Kenny had shook him. He had tried to distract himself, especially after Kenny's death, with rough-housing and sneaking around with Judy and some of the other girls, but now it was too much. All too much. Tears streamed down his face. He shook his head. *I'm nothing*, he thought. *And I'm going to die someday, too, and it will mean nothing.*

Certainly something to think about, but his most pressing issue at the moment was that he had to pee. Badly. His dick felt like a dam threatening to break. Wandering further into the woods, Mike found a tree to piss on.

As he unzipped, planting one hand on the tree to steady himself, he continued to ponder. He wasn't going to die anytime soon, of course. It would be decades before he kicked the bucket.

A thick stream of hot piss came flowing out of him, painting the tree. He moaned in relief.

He would go to college, find a job, get married, raise a family, all that shit. But still, the inevitability of his death bothered him. He didn't want to die. He wanted to live forever.

He continued peeing. It felt like it would never end. When was the last time he took a piss? He couldn't remember.

It was then he realized that someone was standing behind him. Frowning, he turned his head to one side to get a better look. All he could tell from this angle was that it was a girl, short, with long black hair.

"Judy?" he asked.

There was no answer. He shook his head. "Okay, don't answer me." He chuckled, sniffing away his drying tears. "Wanna help me with this? Fucking thing weighs a ton!" Another laugh.

A hand reached under his crotch from behind. Mike raised his eyebrows. He chuckled again. "Didn't think that was gonna work. I was just kidding, you know?"

But Judy—if it *was* Judy—kept her hand down there, though she hadn't touched him yet. What was she doing down there?

There was a brilliant glint of light as Judy's hand moved swiftly between his legs, followed by a flash of pain. His stream of piss halted and he screamed. "Ah!" he said. "What the fuck?"

The piss stream started going again but something was wrong. His hand was wet—the stream was hitting his hand somehow. His dick suddenly felt weightless in his grip. Neither made any sense. Instinctively, he looked down, his mouth dropping open in shock.

Raising his hand, he looked at the severed dick in his palm. He recognized it, of course—it was his own. Whose else could it be? *Please let it be someone else's!* The stream of liquid gushing out of his crotch was no longer piss—it was blood. He had been castrated and now painted the tree with his own gore.

He took a few drunken, panicked steps back from the tree, his open fly spraying blood into the air. The figure behind him stepped aside, and now he could see her. It was Angela.

Angela, her face an insane, wild mask, her eyes impossibly large and wide. Mike opened his mouth to scream. Angela grabbed him by the hair with her free hand and brought the hunting knife up. She plunged it into his gaping mouth, striking upwards with the blade, shattering his palate and driving the weapon into his brain.

Mike remained conscious for a few seconds, his body convulsing, spreading his spray of piss-blood around the forest. Finally, he slumped to the ground and moved no more.

7

The Other Angela opened the door to her bunk and stalked

inside. Her hunting knife dripped blood. It left little tracks on the floor as she approached Judy's bed.

It was dark, but Angela could sense Judy's presence. She knew—simply knew—that the girl was here. But after her eyes adjusted to the dark, she could tell that the girl wasn't asleep in her bed. And yet…

Judy's bed was askew, as if it had been pushed away from the wall for some reason. Angela curiously got down on her hands and knees—stalking style—and looked under the bed. *There you are.* Frowned. Cocked her head to one side.

Judy was already dead. Angela slowly stood up, not understanding what had happened here. Who had killed Judy?

Angela turned and left the bunk. She tried to put the pieces together, but her brain was overwhelmed trying to keep two consciousnesses active at the same time.

She wondered if the person who had killed Judy was the same person who had killed Artie.

8

Ricky headed to the rec hall. He was tired and hungry. Troubling thoughts circled his mind. Madness must run in the family. His mother clearly wasn't quite all there. Some years after his parents had separated, his father had died in a freak accident, leaving Ricky only with his mother. Now, after seeing how Angela was—and how *he* was—Ricky was convinced that his mother had killed his father.

And now he was a killer. Three times over.

He had killed Artie to protect Angela, and no doubt countless other children who would be victimized by that asshole. And he had killed Ben because the old chef had seen him, Ricky, running from the "accident" in the kitchen. But Judy? That had been something else entirely.

Judy had been a bitch to Angela, and plenty of other people at camp, but did she deserve to die for that? Ricky honestly didn't know. Part of him felt that what he had done was justified, while another part of him was deeply ashamed of it, especially how ugly it became. He had no intention of using the curling iron when he went in the bunk—it was there and he simply grabbed it and used it. What did that say about him as a person? And did he even want to think about the answer? It had obviously affected him since he had taken the time to hide the girl's body, half-assed as it was.

His stomach growled. He had barely eaten anything during dinner because it was awful. Now he felt like if he didn't eat he would wither away into nothingness. As he approached the rec hall, a stream of campers was leaving. Gene was on the door and when Ricky started down the stairs to enter, the counselor reached out and grabbed him.

"Wait a minute," Gene said. "Where do you think you're going?"

"Inside," Ricky said, "to get something to eat."

"Oh, no, little man. The social's over. Get back to the bunk."

"Give me a break, huh? I've been lying down all night because dinner made me sick. Just let me grab something real quick."

"Dinner was shitty," Gene said, seeming to consider it. "Just make it snappy."

"Thanks, Geno," Ricky said. He headed inside. Susie was closing things down with a few of the other counselors. She smiled at him as he made his way to the back to grab a few candy bars—all that was left at the end of the night. Ricky had been hoping for cupcakes or some kind of other baked good, but no dice, it seemed.

His meager treasure acquired, Ricky left the rec hall and headed through camp towards his bunk. He unwrapped a candy bar and bit into it as he walked. While it wasn't amazing, it was certainly better than dinner, and it filled his stomach.

About halfway back to his cabin he became aware of someone behind him, just keeping pace with him. When he sped up, his shadow did the same. He felt hands close around his neck.

"What the—" he said before he was dragged into the woods.

"I got you now, you little monster!" Mel said as he manhandled Ricky. "It's your turn."

"Get the fuck off me!" Ricky said.

Mel punched him in the face and the boy went down. The pain was bright and intense. Ricky thought that his nose was broken. Mel stood over him, an accusing finger pointing down.

"You killed them!" he said. "Billy and Kenny! You sick little bastard, you killed Meg!"

That last name made Ricky confused. "What are you talking about?!"

"No excuses! You killed them all!"

The camp owner dropped to his knees, driving one of them into Ricky's stomach and knocking the wind out of him. He punched Ricky again, this time in the left eye.

"I didn't kill Meg!" Ricky managed to scream through the pain.

"Liar!" Mel said.

He punched and punched and punched. Each hit felt like a baseball bat to Ricky. He heard multiple cracks and crunches, felt blood fill up his mouth. His lungs. Trying to defend himself, he kicked out and landed a good knee into Mel's crotch.

The old camp owner clutched his balls and rolled off Ricky. The boy turned over, trying to crawl towards the path.

"Help!" he shouted, but the path seemed miles away. Pain surged through his body with every tiny bit of movement.

Soon, Mel was back, grabbing Ricky by his feet and yanking him back into the woods. The camp owner twisted the boy's right ankle and forced him to turn onto his back once again. There was a crack as something in his foot broke. Mel stomped on his lower leg and that broke, too. Now all that Ricky could do was scream.

After another moment, he couldn't even do that, anymore.

Mel stomped on his jaw, dislodging it. His nose came next. A final stomp on Ricky's neck sealed the boy's fate, breaking his trachea. He couldn't breathe.

As Ricky began to lose consciousness, his final thoughts were of Angela. Though some part of him had hoped that his final moments were serene, and only full of good tidings, the reality was that in his last moments he hoped Angela killed every single person in camp.

Ricky died with hate in his heart.

CHAPTER
TEN

LAST CHANCE AT THE
WATERFRONT

1

Marie was enjoying a cigarette outside her cabin. The minute she saw Ronnie coming, she pitched it away and tried to dissipate the smoke by blowing and waving. Ronnie looked like he had other things on his mind. In fact, he looked deeply troubled.

"I need you to get all the counselors together," Ronnie said. "Meet me at my shack."

"What?" Marie said. "Why?"

Ronnie shook his head. "I just talked to Eddie. At least four kids are dead."

"Dead?"

"Murdered."

"Jesus."

"Now get everybody together," Ronnie said. "Right now!"

He took off, heading towards his shack. Marie got going. Susie had been right—there was a murderer at Camp Arawak. She could hardly believe it. Were they all in danger? Who would be next?

2

When Angela emerged from the cover of heavy trees and approached Ricky's body, she didn't know what she was seeing at first. Her cousin had been pummeled so badly that Angela didn't recognize him. His face, especially, was a mask of dark red blood. Under the blood, the boy's features had been twisted out of shape, beaten by frantic, enraged adult hands. One of Ricky's eyes had been utterly destroyed. It had been punched so hard the orb had been pushed into the boy's mulch. His nose was much the same, beaten until it had simply collapsed into his skull. His jaw hung loose, broken on one side—the left. Ricky looked like an action figure that had been chewed on by a dog.

Angela dropped to her knees beside the body—he was dead, she knew that—and felt tears streaming down her face. But the Other Angela, the one deep inside, wouldn't let her mourn. That Other Angela wanted revenge, swift and brutal.

Kill him, kill him, kill him! she demanded inside Angela's head.

She looked up, the Other totally in control now, and watched as Mel retreated towards the general direction of the cabins. The camp owner looked like a scared rabbit. His horrible, violent deed done, the man had reverted to his cowardly, weaselly self once more.

Angela grit her teeth and got up. She was in much better shape than Mel, who never seemed to be without a cigar, and was obviously far younger. Catching up to him would be no challenge at all. She ran after him but gave him some breathing room. Let him think that he had gotten away from this awful act.

Angela gave him a wide berth, got ahead of him. By the time the old man reached the archery range—coughing and winded—the girl was waiting for him.

3

Mel couldn't quite believe what he had done. As he made his way through the woods, his mind was a rush of confused, frantic thoughts. Had he really killed that boy? It didn't seem possible, but he was sure that it was true. He had left Ricky Thomas dead in the woods. On the very ground he owned.

He shut these morbid thoughts out, pushed them aside like so much trash. He had done it for Meg. To avenge her death. And all that mattered now was making sure that he got away with it. The boy was nothing—*rich* nothing but nothing all the same—and Mel was not going to be put down by a foul-mouthed little nothing. This was nothing but a setback, no more than that. He would emerge unscathed, as he always did. He was nothing if not slippery.

Emerging from the thick woods into an open field, he could see the cabins ahead of him. A momentary feeling of relief washed over him and a smile played around his lips. *Almost home.*

That's when he saw the figure.

It took him a moment to even decide the gender of the figure. *Female.* It was a girl. One of the campers. What was she doing out here this late, after the social? There was a killer at large!

But, of course, that wasn't true. Not anymore. He had put the killer down with his own hands. This made him feel good again, offsetting how startled he had been.

The girl stood about fifty yards away from him just out of the moonlight in the shadow of a tree. She held something in her hands. Two somethings, in fact, but he couldn't quite tell what they were.

The girl stepped out of the shadow, and Mel finally recognized her. It was Angela Baker, Ricky's weirdo cousin. The quiet one.

"No," Mel said.

Angela twirled one of the somethings that she held in one hand, rolling it between her thumb and the first two fingers of her hand. The moonlight glinted off one end of the object and Mel finally figured out what it was.

It was an arrow.

And all of a sudden he knew where he was. This wasn't just any old field. This was the archery range. The girl had three more arrows stuck into the ground beside her.

He looked into Angela's mad-but-placid face and the revelation hit him all at once. Seeing her here in the dark, he knew—simply *knew*—that she was the killer. The real killer. Mel still believed that Ricky had attacked Artie but the others? Those belonged to Angela.

Still, his animal brain wouldn't accept the truth. "It can't be!"

Angela brought the arrow together with the object she held in her other hand, a bow. Nocked it.

Mel seemed incapable of movement. He was locked in place. It was all too much—the murder of Ricky, the realization that Angela was the actual killer, the almost-certain loss of his camp and the financial burden that would follow—and he only seemed capable of a definitive, pathetic, shout: "It can't be you!"

They turned out to be his final words.

Angela let go of the arrow. As it sailed through the air towards him, Mel had time to articulate one last, absurd thought: *It's the only thing she's good at around Camp Arawak. Susie told me about her. The little bitch can really make those arrows fly!*

The arrow penetrated his neck and went all the way through, emerging from the nape of his neck, the tip dripping blood. Instantly, breath seemed impossible. Blood filled his throat and he coughed as a wave of the stuff flooded his mouth. He gurgled hideously as blood trailed from either side of his jaw. He reached out for the arrow with both hands. It was a reflex—a useless one. What was he going to do, pull it out?

Angela already had her second arrow nocked and sent it

flying. The projectile struck his left shoulder and stuck fast in the muscle and fat. His arm fell limp to his side, the nerves no longer responding to his brain. More blood drooled from his mouth.

Instinct took over, and Mel tried to get away. He turned in place, pain shooting through his entire body, intending to head back into the woods, but he never made it. Angela let loose with another arrow. Mel had reached out to the woods with his good right arm, a pathetic gesture, like a small child reaching out for his mother, and the arrow hit him in the right armpit.

Agony and a mouthful of blood cascaded from him. It arced through the air, glinting in the moonlight, like Angela's twirling arrow, before splashing to the earth at Mel's feet.

Struggling to move once again, Mel's brain shut down bit by bit, like a guard switching off the lights in an old factory. The man was quite the sight. One arm hanging useless at his side, the other thrust out like a mummy in a 1940s movie, three arrows stuck in him like a voodoo doll.

Mel hadn't been able to breathe for almost a full minute now. He was dying and he knew it. The lack of oxygen was intoxicating in a poisonous kind of way. He could see black bugs crawling in at the edges of his vision.

In his last moments, he saw everything with crystal clarity. Saw the cabins beyond Angela. So close yet so far, as if they were taunting him. Saw the girl nocking her final arrow and taking aim. She looked like a wild animal, like some kind of monster in a children's story, the kind told around the campfire in the dog days of summer.

The kind of story told at *his* campground.

Angela let the final arrow go, and it took Mel in the left knee. He didn't think he could feel anymore pain, but here it was, acute in a way he had never felt before.

Mel's jaw dropped open as this final, painful wave crashed over him. His chin hit the shaft of the arrow in his neck and sent yet another shock of pain through him. This time he did fall, landing on his back. The arrow in his neck twisted to one side, tearing out of his throat as it snapped and shattered.

Mel began to shake and writhe in abject pain as the life bled out of his body in rivulets. Angela approached him slowly. The final thing that Mel saw, before the black bugs entirely covered his field of vision, was her animal face leering over him. Her eyes were wide and wild. She looked like she was going to eat him. Then he could see no more and there was only darkness and pain.

It took him several more agonizing minutes to die.

4

Officer Frank Breton pulled into Camp Arawak and headed directly to Ronnie's shack. Kenny's autopsy had come back this evening, and it was clear that it had been no accident. And now this frantic phone call from the camp.

There was already a group of counselors waiting for him. Ronnie pushed through them to meet the police officer.

"I filled them all in," he said.

The police officer nodded. "Good." He addressed the assembled group of counselors at large. "Ronnie and I will begin searching the cabins. I suggest the rest of you return to your charges, and make sure they're all present and accounted for."

Susie joined Ronnie's side, shook her head. "I can't find Angela or Judy."

"Has anyone seen Meg?" Marie asked.

"Or Mel?" Hal said.

There was a chorus of shaking heads. Ronnie frowned. "They were supposed to be going out tonight. They're probably together in his shack."

There were several surprised looks. Ronnie waved them away. "Get back to your bunks and make sure nobody leaves. There's a killer on the loose! Got it?"

Before any of them could properly answer, Gene came

running out of the dark and joined the rest of them. "Paul and Ricky haven't come back yet. I saw Ricky when the social was ending, but he's not in his bunk. Same thing with Paul."

One of the other counselors, Jeff, pushed aside Gene. "Mike, either. Haven't seen him at all."

"Jesus Christ," Ronnie said.

"Alright," Officer Breton said. "We're gonna form into teams. Gene, you come with me. We'll search the woods. Ronnie, and is it Susie?"

Susie nodded.

"You two start searching the cabins," the officer said. "Even the empty ones. And for God's sake, be careful. Everybody else, take care of the rest of the kids. And don't scare them."

They started to break into groups. Just as Marie was starting to head back to her bunk, Susie stopped her, grabbing her gently by the arm. They looked at each other. Shared a quick but heartfelt kiss. Several of the counselors appeared to be shocked.

"Be careful," Susie said when the kiss broke. Marie nodded.

After that, they all left Ronnie's shack. Four of them went looking for a killer.

5

Angela decided that Paul had one last chance. He had already left her to fend for herself twice in the face of Meg's bullying, and he had stepped out with Judy, making out with her behind Angela's back. The Other Angela wanted him dead, and it took every ounce of willpower from Angela to stop her. Because she could tell that Paul liked her—really liked her— and she wanted to give him a chance to redeem himself.

He was already waiting for her when she arrived, freshly showered. Her hair was a little frizzy by this point in the night. It gave her a wild, animalistic look—the Other Angela just peeking out from behind the mask.

She approached him silently as he wandered around the

bleachers until coming to rest and sitting down at what Angela considered "her spot" on the front bench. Finally, when she was less than three feet away from him, Paul spotted her. Smiled.

"I didn't think you were gonna show," he said.

Without answering him—in words, anyway—Angela sat down next to him on the bench. Reached out and took his hand in hers. They looked at each other. Paul was still smiling.

He was cute. No, more than cute: handsome. When he leaned in for a kiss, she let him, and kissed him back. It was a good kiss, and a long one. When it was over, she looked out at the water, and he did the same. They spent a serene moment together just looking out at the water and not talking. Hands still locked together.

"Let's go swimming," Angela said.

"Now?" Paul said. "What about our clothes?"

She only hesitated for a moment before answering. "Take them off."

She wasn't looking at his face when he responded, but she could hear the excitement in his voice. "OK!"

She heard him unbuttoning his shirt as she stood up, beginning to do the same. Taking a few steps out towards the water, she shrugged out of her shirt and tossed it as far out in the waves as she could. *Won't be needing that anymore.*

She kicked off her shoes and into the water they went. Down came her pants. Her underwear. When she was completely nude, she covered herself, one hand across her chest, the other over her crotch. She kept her eyes on the lake and thought she could see a water snake slithering near the shore. A tear ran down her cheeks as she prepared to turn around and face Paul.

Last chance.

She held her breath and turned around. Paul was just finishing getting undressed. He was bent over, mooning her, as he folded his clothes neatly on the bench. When he turned around, he had a big smile on his face.

Angela dropped both arms to her sides and exposed herself

to him. She had expected surprise, shock even, and she wasn't disappointed. Paul stared at her body, his mouth slack-jawed. Shock turned to horror, revulsion, and he clapped both hands over his mouth.

Angela felt a string of emotions all at once: anger, fear, disgust, rage, disappointment. Sadness. Tears still wet on her face, Angela reached down and grabbed something out of her jeans, the only piece of her clothing left on the beach. When she stood up, object in hand, and started towards Paul, Angela and the Other Angela were one at last.

The *new* Angela smiled. It was wide, full of teeth, and quite insane.

6

Susie stood outside the empty bunk, a hand over her mouth. Ronnie was still inside, waving his flashlight around to see if he could find anything else. There was nothing more, Susie was quite sure of it.

They had just discovered Meg's body, chopped up and stuffed into the cubicle over a bed. It was horrible. Although Meg wasn't exactly a nice person, Susie had got along with her pretty well all the years they had been working at Camp Arawak together. To see her now, murdered and mutilated, was a shock.

Ronnie stepped out of the cabin, shaking his head. He had been rattled, Susie could tell. Still, he put a hand on Susie's shoulder.

"Are you alright?" he asked.

Susie dropped the hand from her mouth. Nodded. "Yeah, I think so."

"That's all the empty cabins," he said. "Marie and the others will be checking the occupied bunks." He shook his head.

"What about that rundown shack just outside camp?" Susie asked.

"Gene and Officer Breton can check that," Ronnie said.

"They're on the other side of camp."

Slowly, Ronnie nodded. "Alright. Let's go."

They made their way through camp until they reached an old, abandoned shack on the outskirts of the property. Susie could already smell something rank as they approached it. Ronnie had his flashlight pointed out ahead of him like a crucifix wielded against a vampire. The two of them reached the shack's main door. Shared a look.

There was no lock—it had been broken off long ago—so Ronnie used his flashlight to push the door open. A strong breeze came in behind them and slammed the door inward. It rattled on its rusty hinges. Once it settled, Susie could hear movement inside the shack. Skittering, crawling, the buzzing of flies. The smell was overpowering, and Susie covered her mouth and nose.

Ronnie's flashlight explored the darkness. Neither of them made a move to enter the dark, abandoned shack. The beam penetrated the blackness, and Susie saw a rat scurrying away. Soon, she saw a nest of cockroaches do much the same.

Then the maggots.

There were hundreds of them feasting on a mound of flesh on the floor. It was a dead body.

"Jesus Christ," Ronnie said. "Who is it?"

"I think it's Ben," Susie said.

"Oh my God."

After another sweep with the flashlight, they decided that there was no one else inside, and headed well away from the shack. Susie coughed a few times and resisted the urge to vomit.

"What now?" Ronnie said.

Susie shook her head. "I don't know."

"We could be going about this all wrong."

"What do you mean?"

"We're both thinking that all these kids have been killed," Ronnie said.

"God, I hope not," Susie said.

"But that's what's in your head, right?"

"Right."

"What if they're just being kids, and they don't know they're in danger? What if they're just out fooling around?"

"Okay," Susie said. "I see what you mean."

"So where would kids go to fool around at night around here?" Ronnie asked.

Susie nodded, looked through the trees towards camp. "The waterfront."

"Yeah, the waterfront. So that's where we go."

The two of them headed in that direction, picking up the pace. Susie hoped they would find Angela, at least, alive. That girl had been through enough this summer.

7

"Who would do that to someone, officer?" Gene asked.

The two of them were on the archery field. Gene shined his flashlight down at Mel's arrow-riddled body. There was one in the man's shoulder, another in his armpit, another in his knee, one in his neck and about ten driven into his face. Gene thought that at least some of them had been stuck in the man after he was already dead.

"A madman," Officer Breton said. He was also looking down at the body, a reflexive expression on his face. "There was a nut who killed a few people near North Sea Cottages in Jersey a little while ago." He raised the flashlight beam to Gene's face. "They never caught him."

"You don't think..." Gene trailed off.

"I don't know. All I know is that I've never seen anything like this before. Not firsthand, anyway."

Neither of them said anything for a moment. Finally, Gene

gestured towards the woods nearby. "Let's keep looking, alright?"

Officer Breton nodded, and they left Mel's body behind. Not far into the woods, they came across another body. Gene spotted it first, from a distance. He pointed it out, and the two of them made their way towards it.

As they were making their way through the trees, Gene stepped on something soft and fleshy. Thinking that it must have been a slug, Gene screwed up his face and wiped the creature off his boot on a nearby tree stump. What was left behind on the stump was not a slug.

Gene reared back in horror at the severed penis that he just stepped on.

Officer Breton took a look at the appendage, winced, and went on to the body. It was slumped on the ground, and the police officer turned it over. Nodded. "Looks like it came off this young man. You know him?"

Gene, still biting his lower lip and thinking about the severed dick, took a look at the body. "Yeah. That's Mike. Jesus, look what they did to him." He gestured to the penis.

Officer Breton nodded again. They continued on their way, and after a while they came upon a few candy bars on the forest ground. Following the trail deeper in the woods, they found the body of a boy that had been beaten and stomped to death. Once more, the police officer asked the young counselor if he knew the identity of the corpse.

Gene nodded, tears already in his eyes. He dropped to his knees beside Ricky Thomas' body and shook his head in despair. Reached out to the corpse but couldn't bear to touch it.

He began to cry and shut down completely, weeping into his hands. It took Officer Breton some time to get him up and mobile once again.

8

Marie heard the girls screaming before she reached the cabin. Rushing inside, she could smell something awful: a mixture of singed hair and burnt flesh. Girls came streaming out of the bunk as she looked around to see what was wrong. One of them pointed at one of the beds in the corner of the room.

Marie approached the bed. There was a curling iron, still plugged in, on the ground near the bed. Marie could see a pair of legs sticking out from behind the bed on the floor.

With caution, and mounting horror, Marie walked up to the bed, and pushed it aside to get a good look.

Judy's dead, open eyes stared up at her. The girl was no more, but her eyes were just as mean and striking. Marie covered her mouth with both hands and screamed.

Running from the bunk and into the chill night air, she ran straight into Officer Breton and Gene, who had just returned from their search of the woods. Rushing into Gene's arms, the two counselors cried together. Officer Breton went into the bunk to see for himself. He came out dazed and overwhelmed.

When Marie had enough of her wits back to speak, she looked at the police officer, then up at Gene. "Where's Susie?"

In all the confusion, no one noticed a car pull into camp.

9

"Angela! Ricky! Paul!"

Susie and Ronnie made as much noise as they could while approaching the lake, wanting to make sure everyone knew where they were. Perhaps if the killer was still at large, he would be scared away. One could hope, at least.

Ronnie's flashlight sputtered, flickered, and went out. "Damn!" He smacked it. The flashlight flickered, then went dark. Ronnie tossed the useless thing aside. Then he stopped short. Susie looked at him.

"What?" she asked.

"You hear that?" he said. "Sounds like singing."

Susie listened and, yes, she could hear it. Someone humming off-key. Susie was reminded of her mother humming to herself while doing various tasks around the house. It brought back her childhood in a way that surprised her.

Shaking it off, she and Ronnie proceeded onto the beach around the lake. The humming was coming from the other side of the bleachers, near the water. Rounding the bleachers, the two of them came upon someone sitting on the ground, facing away from them, looking out towards water, and another lying their head on the sitting person's lap.

"Angela?" Susie said.

There wasn't a lot of moonlight, and they had trouble seeing, but it did appear to be Angela who was sitting on the sand, humming to herself. And that could be Paul lying on the ground, his head in her lap. They were both naked.

Susie breathed a sigh of relief. Obviously, Ronnie had been right. Angela and Paul had snuck away after the social, off to the waterfront to fool around.

They're alive, Susie thought. "Angela!" was what she said.

At the utterance of her name, Angela quickly stood up, grabbing something that had been sitting in the sand by her side. As she stood, she jostled Paul. He rolled away from her towards the water.

But not all of him.

His severed head dropped from Angela's lap as she stood, and it rolled towards them. Ronnie yelped in terror. "Jesus Christ!"

Angela turned, a hunting knife in one hand, her naked body covered in blood. It was splattered across her chest and stomach, and traced down her arms and legs. Her face was a mask of pure animal rage. Susie didn't see a little girl in there, only a predator ready to strike.

But something else was off. Susie frowned. Was that…?

Angela had a penis. Susie was confused. What was she looking at? Ronnie articulated it for her.

"How can it be?" he said. "She's a boy."

10

*Boy? **Boy?!***

She wasn't a boy. Why would Ronnie call her that? Was he stupid? Crazy? Angela might have been different, but she was no boy. Pure rage built up inside her.

I'll show them. I'll show them that I'm not someone you can bully! I'll show them all!

Angela—the *new* Angela—growled at Susie and Ronnie, her knife raised, and started towards them. Both of the counselors backed away in fear.

"Angela!" a voice cried out from the direction of camp. "There's my little angel!"

Angela stopped dead in her tracks. Turned towards the voice. Dropped the knife. It landed in the sand with a thunk. Angela stared in shock as Aunt Martha walked towards her out of the darkness, arms outstretched, ready to take her in an embrace.

Angela rushed towards her aunt and accepted the hug. Her aunt didn't seem to mind that her clothes were now getting all bloody and dirty. She just seemed glad to see her little angel once again.

"You look a terrible fright, my dear!" Aunt Martha said. "When Richard called me yesterday, he seemed so awfully distressed that I came up here the very moment that I could spare! Yes, that's just what I did. The very second that I wasn't needed at my practice." She seemed to notice the two counselors for the first time. "I am a doctor, you know?"

Ronnie nodded. Susie only looked on in shock and worry. She put out a warning hand.

"Be careful, ma'am," she said. "We... We don't know what happened here."

"I can see for myself what happened," Aunt Martha said. "My poor little angel was scared, and she defended herself." She looked down at Angela. "I let you go to camp too early, didn't I, Angela?"

Angela found herself nodding into her aunt's chest. Her eyes were wide open and staring out into the darkness.

"Yes, too early," Aunt Martha said. "Richard so wanted you to come along. And anything that my Richard wants, he gets." She looked at the counselors once again. "Some would say that I spoil them, but they're the only children I have." She then looked off into nothingness. "Yes, after my husband left." Seemed to restart, like a computer booting up. "He had an accident.

Years ago now. No longer with us, you understand."

Angela looked up at her aunt. *Accident.* Like Artie the cook. Angela started to piece it together. It was Ricky who had killed Artie. And probably Judy, too. Ricky had been like her, like Angela.

And they were both like Aunt Martha. And her grandfather.

Angela had heard the stories of her grandfather, Peter, before but never really believed them. Now, though, she was certain that she had been caught in a legacy of madness. A labyrinth that she was too young, too sheltered, to navigate.

"What manner of camp is this?" Aunt Martha said. "Accidents, murders? Can it be true? Do the proper authorities know?" A look of concern on her face.

"I..." Ronnie said, trailing off.

"You did this to me," Angela said. It was a whisper.

"What was that, my little angel?"

"You made me someone that I wasn't."

"I don't know what you mean, dear."

But she did know. Angela could see it in her crazy face. She knew, she remembered. Remembered making Angela take on the persona of her own dead sister. She wouldn't let Angela be the kind of girl she wanted to be, the girl she was meant to be.

Wouldn't let her be her own person.

Angela grit her teeth and began to hiss like a snake. She started to shake. Convulse.

"What ever is the matter, my little angel?" Aunt Martha said.

"Ma'am," Ronnie said, "maybe you should let go of her."

"I am her legal guardian," Aunt Martha said with a forced laugh. "I will not let her go. She needs to be protected."

"I think she can take care of herself," Susie said.

Angela's hiss got louder, more hostile. Aunt Martha gazed down at her and looked genuinely worried for the first time. She looked up, craning her neck, to the counselors.

"You know," she said, "perhaps I shou—"

That was as far as she got. Angela struck like a snake, darting her head up and forward, teeth locking onto her aunt's exposed neck. It only took a moment to bite through the carotid artery, but Angela kept going, gnawing at the muscle and tendons beneath.

Blood fountained as Aunt Martha screamed. She beat on her niece's back, but it did no good. Angela wouldn't let go. She ate through her aunt's neck like an animal.

Soon, gore and viscera joined the blood and Aunt Martha collapsed onto her back. Angela went down with her aunt, her hair now drenched red. Blood ran down her back.

Hearing the screaming and the shouts, Officer Breton, Marie, Gene, and several other counselors came running to the lake. It took five of them to tear Angela off her aunt. By then, the woman was dead.

Angela was hissing and screaming when they pulled her off. She was completely covered in blood and shrieking like a demon from the depths of Hell.

EPILOGUE
A FIELD TRIP

That had been years ago.

Angela was better now. All the doctors at the mental facility said so. They said she was a model patient, which was high praise coming from them. They had helped facilitate her transition over the years, as well. It was what Angela had wanted.

And now, they had let her go on this little field trip to the former grounds of Camp Arawak, long since abandoned. She was supervised, of course. An orderly named Claude had driven her out here today to keep an eye on her.

There were still bullies in the world. Even when everything seemed to be going well, they were still around to cause people pain. Claude was one of them. He treated Angela like trash or something that he had stepped on. Angela didn't like him.

Not one bit.

Finally ready to leave the ruins of the camp, Angela lingered near the van which would bring her back to the mental facility. It was big, bulky, and white, like they all were. Claude was sitting in the driver's seat, ready to go.

Angela leaned against the van beside the driver's side door. Sighed. All she wanted to do was remake her own childhood. She wanted to spend her adult life at camp and really enjoy herself this time. But that would never happen, she supposed. She would never be let out of the mental facility.

"I'm ready to leave," she said to Claude.

When he didn't answer, she turned to him. The driver's side window was rolled down, and she leaned into it, resting her arms on it.

"Tired, Claude?" she asked. "Want me to drive?" Still no answer. "Great! I can do that. I know how to: got some lessons! Here, move aside."

She opened the driver's side door, giving the big man some space to leave. When the door was fully open, Claude tumbled out of the van and hit the asphalt. An old arrow had been driven into his right temple.

Angela looked down at him. "Oh, you want to stay here? Sure. I won't tell anyone. You enjoy yourself."

She stepped over him and got into the van. With a smile, she started up the vehicle and drove off. There were all manner of campgrounds in the tri-state area.

Why, with enough time, she could visit them all if she wanted to!

A fan made Sleepaway Camp *poster that has circulated the internet for years.*
Artist Unknown.

The following image gallery contains images from Sleepaway Camp. Used by permission.

SLEEPAWAY CAMP

...you won't be
coming home!

UNITED FILM DISTRIBUTION COMPANY Presents "SLEEPAWAY CAMP"

Starring MIKE KELLIN · KATHERINE KAMHI · PAUL De ANGELO

Co-Starring JONATHAN TIERSTON · FELISSA ROSE · CHRISTOPHER COLLET

KAREN FIELDS Executive Producer ROBERT HILTZIK Music by EDWARD BILOUS

Produced by MICHELE TATOSIAN and JERRY SILVA Written and Directed by ROBERT HILTZIK

© 1983 AMERICAN EAGLE FILMS CORP.   R RESTRICTED   Released By

Dear Mom and Dad,
I've been at Sleepaway Camp
for almost three weeks now
and I'm getting very scared
all the kids are all getting

VIDEOMAT
2298
-3

SLEEPAWAY
CAMP

A Nice Place For Summer Vacation.
A Perfect Place To Die!

CAMP
FOR SALE
ARAWAK

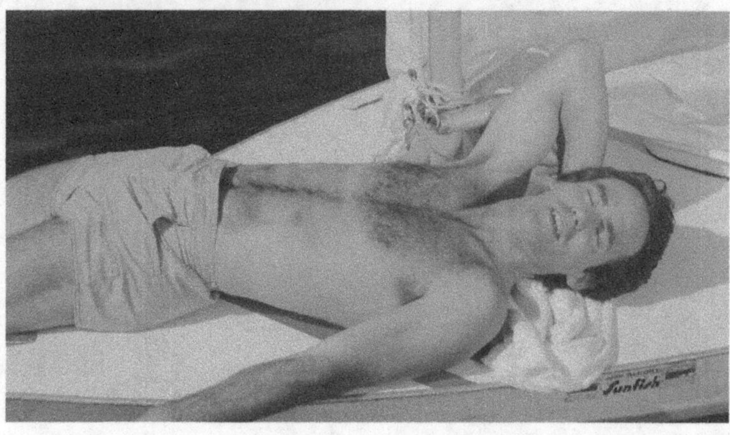
Sunfish

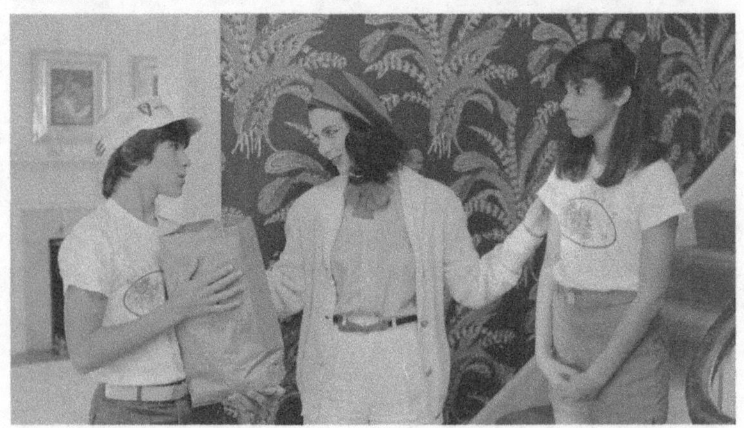

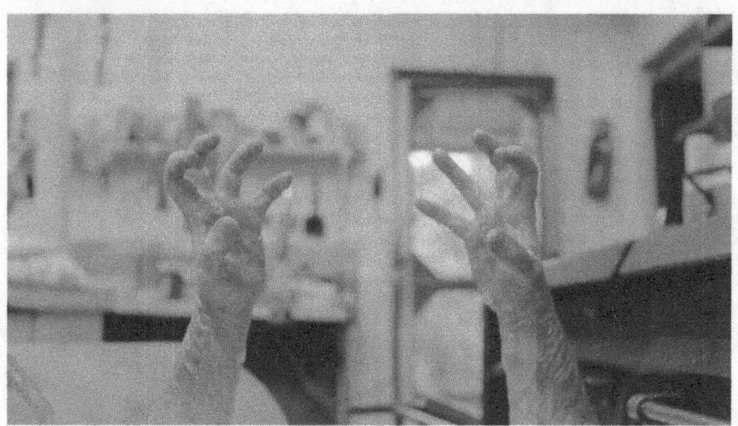

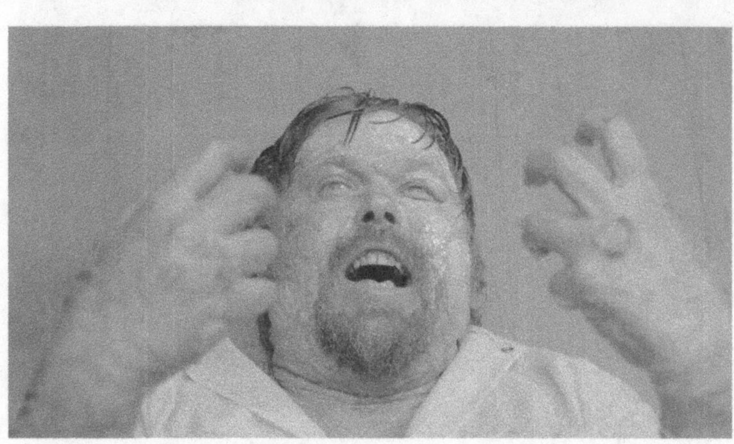

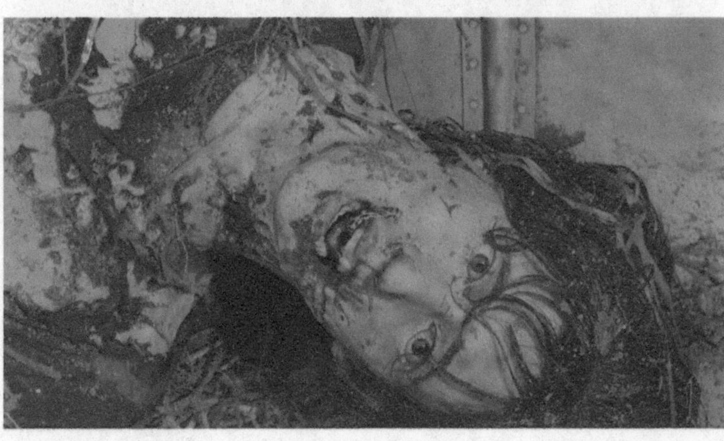

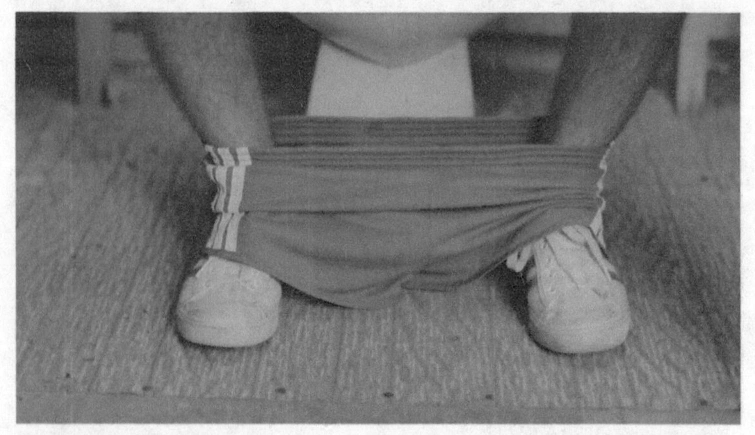

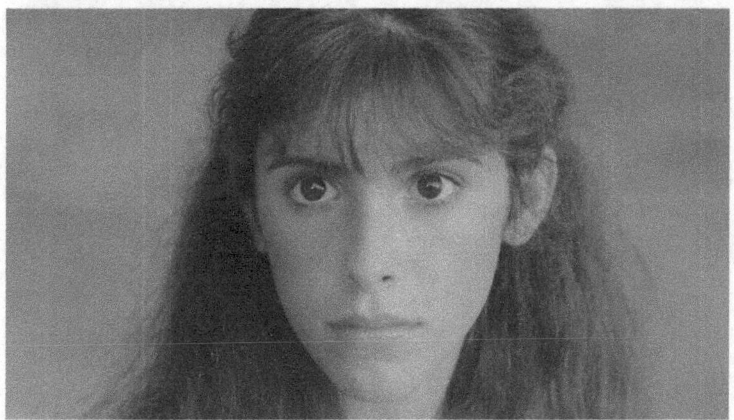

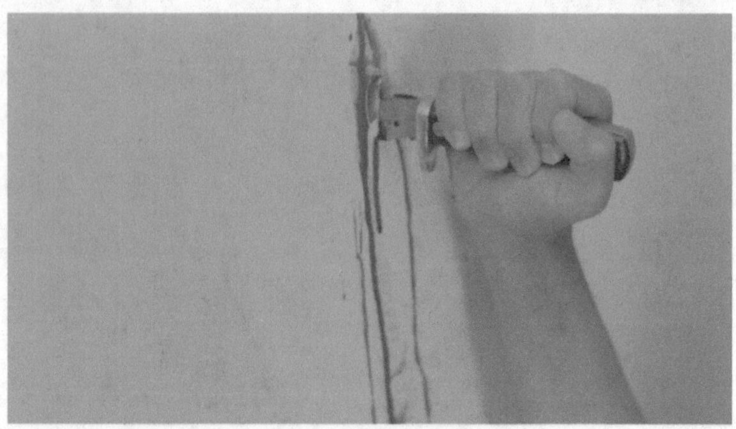

ACKNOWLEDGMENTS

A book is never truly written in isolation - not at least if it is ever intended for publication - and I have a lot of people to thank for bringing this particular book to light and life: Robert Hiltzik, who wrote and directed the film, *Sleepaway Camp*, and without whom, we wouldn't be here right now; the cast and crew of *Sleepaway Camp*, especially Felissa Rose, who embodied Angela Baker so brilliantly; Jeff Hayes, for keeping the campfire lit; the Wives Colangelo, for keen insight, even if I strayed from the path they laid out (please forgive me!); my family and friends, who supported me during the writing process; Amanda Duron and Amy Vorhees Searles from Severin, for giving me the push; Mark Miller and Sean Duregger of Encyclopocalypse - Sean for keeping the rest of us separated from any pesky money issues, Mark for his kindness and brilliant editing skills; and, finally, Brendan Hargous, Lucas Tizzano, Jason Duron, Jaron Carr, and Aaron Hudson, for reading the book in manuscript form and providing feedback and constructive criticism. You're all great!

ABOUT THE AUTHOR

B.R. Flynn is a trans author who lives, works, and writes in Arizona.

RECOMMENDED READING

Sleepaway Camp **by BJ and Harmony Colangelo**

Nonfiction | DieDieBooks

www.diediebooks.com

BJ & Harmony Colangelo assess where *Sleepaway Camp* falls in
the slasher canon and do a deep dive on the film's themes and
legacy, exploring how changing attitudes towards the LGBT
community has led to both a reclamation and necessary critique
of the film by modern audiences.